Tunnel

Books by Vernon Coleman include:

The Medicine Men (1975)
Paper Doctors (1976)
Stress Control (1978)
The Home Pharmacy (1980)
Aspirin or Ambulance (1980)
Face Values (1981)
The Good Medicine Guide (1982)
Bodypower (1983)
Thomas Winsden's Cricketing Almanack (1983)
Diary of a Cricket Lover (1984)
Bodysense (1984)
Life Without Tranquillisers (1985)
The Story Of Medicine (1985, 1998)
Mindpower (1986)
Addicts and Addictions (1986)
Dr Vernon Coleman's Guide To Alternative Medicine (1988)
Stress Management Techniques (1988)
Know Yourself (1988)
The Health Scandal (1988)
The 20 Minute Health Check (1989)
Sex For Everyone (1989)
Mind Over Body (1989)
Eat Green Lose Weight (1990)
How To Overcome Toxic Stress (1990)
Why Animal Experiments Must Stop (1991)
The Drugs Myth (1992)
Complete Guide To Sex (1993)
How to Conquer Backache (1993)
How to Conquer Pain (1993)
Betrayal of Trust (1994)
Know Your Drugs (1994, 1997)
Food for Thought (1994, revised edition 2000)
The Traditional Home Doctor (1994)
People Watching (1995)
Relief from IBS (1995)
The Parent's Handbook (1995)
Men in Dresses (1996)
Power over Cancer (1996)
Crossdressing (1996)
How to Conquer Arthritis (1996)
High Blood Pressure (1996)
How To Stop Your Doctor Killing You (1996, revised edition 2003)
Fighting For Animals (1996)
Alice and Other Friends (1996)

Spiritpower (1997)
How To Publish Your Own Book (1999)
How To Relax and Overcome Stress (1999)
Animal Rights – Human Wrongs (1999)
Superbody (1999)
Complete Guide to Life (2000)
Strange But True (2000)
Daily Inspirations (2000)
Stomach Problems: Relief At Last (2001)
How To Overcome Guilt (2001)
How To Live Longer (2001)
Sex (2001)
We Love Cats (2002)
England Our England (2002)
Rogue Nation (2003)
People Push Bottles Up Peaceniks (2003)
The Cats' Own Annual (2003)
Confronting The Global Bully (2004)
Saving England (2004)
Why Everything Is Going To Get Worse Before It Gets Better (2004)
The Secret Lives of Cats (2004)
The Cat Basket (2005)

novels
The Village Cricket Tour (1990)
The Bilbury Chronicles (1992)
Bilbury Grange (1993)
Mrs Caldicot's Cabbage War (1993)
Bilbury Revels (1994)
Deadline (1994)
The Man Who Inherited a Golf Course (1995)
Bilbury Pie (1995)
Bilbury Country (1996)
Second Innings (1999)
Around the Wicket (2000)
It's Never Too Late (2001)
Paris In My Springtime (2002)
Mrs Caldicot's Knickerbocker Glory (2003)
Too Many Clubs And Not Enough Balls (2005)
Tunnel (1980, 2005)

as Edward Vernon
Practice Makes Perfect (1977)
Practise What You Preach (1978)
Getting Into Practice (1979)
Aphrodisiacs – An Owner's Manual (1983)

with Alice

Alice's Diary (1989)
Alice's Adventures (1992)

With Donna Antoinette Coleman

How To Conquer Health Problems Between Ages 50 and 120 (2003)
Health Secrets Doctors Share With Their Families (2005)

Tunnel

Vernon Coleman

Great Fiction

Published by Great Fiction, Publishing House, Trinity Place, Barnstaple, Devon EX32 9HG, England.

First published by Robert Hale in 1980

ISBN: 1-904001-02-5

A catalogue record for this book is available from the British Library.

Dedication

To Donna Antoinette, the Welsh Princess, who caught a later train and arrived in my life some time after I wrote this book. With all my love.

Note

All characters, organisations, businesses in this publication are fictitious and any resemblance to real persons, living or dead, is purely coincidental. This book was written and first published before the existing Channel Tunnel was built and indeed, before the route had been decided and plans for the tunnel approved.

Preface

This novel was written in the late 1970s and first published in 1980 – before the final plans for the Channel Tunnel were drawn up and long before the tunnel was built. When researching the book I spent some time trying to work out where the tunnel should start, where it should end and what form it should take. I am delighted that the tunnel which was eventually built (after millions of pounds of research) bore a notable resemblance to the tunnel I 'designed' and 'built' for this novel.

I should also point out that although an early version of the European Union appears in this book, represented by a character called Susan Roberts, the EU was then still masquerading under one of its earlier pseudonyms and was far less well known for interfering in daily life than it is now.

I wrote *Tunnel* under a pen name because my literary agent at the time didn't think it was the sort of book I should be writing (I had just begun to establish a reputation as an author of hard-hitting medical books such as *The Medicine Men* and *Paper Doctors* and was already writing light, humorous fiction under the pen name Edward Vernon). So the book was first published by Robert Hale under the pen name Marc Charbonnier.

I should also point out that I got round the difference in times between Britain and the continent by publishing a small note at the beginning of the book stating that: 'All the times in this book are given according to European Standard Time (1983 Brussels agreement).' Rather to my surprise, and much to my delight, the EU still hasn't managed to get the clocks sorted out.

Finally, I should mention that since the Channel Tunnel opened for business, and despite what happens in this novel, I have used Eurostar approximately once a month to travel to France.

Vernon Coleman, April 2005

PART ONE

0830 hrs. August 4th, place de la Concorde, Paris

The minibus had stopped in a no-waiting area in the place de la Concorde, Paris, and the driver, a nervous, thin young man with a beard and shoulder-length hair was very agitated. He kept asking the passengers to hurry up and get out so that he could move on. People continued jumping down from the bus long after the normal load had been exceeded. It was difficult to believe so many passengers could have huddled in such cramped quarters, let alone that they could have travelled from Athens together.

The last passenger had more difficulty than the others in leaving the minibus. Whereas they were all dressed in jeans and sweat shirts and carried knapsacks and bedrolls, she was dressed in a well-worn black overcoat and carried a small brown suitcase. On top of her greying hair there perched a small pink hat. Miss Ruby Millington, who was slightly more than 70 years old, was 44 years older than the oldest of her travelling companions. A young man and his female companion helped Miss Millington down the last step, the young man taking her suitcase as she lowered herself to the ground. When she was safely on the pavement, the driver of the minibus let in the clutch and accelerated away amidst the hectic Paris traffic. A horn blared as a taxi travelling too fast had to brake to allow the minibus to join the traffic flow.

Miss Millington had joined the group of young travellers outside the American Express offices in Athens. She had travelled to Greece with a charter group and had been due to spend two nights in Athens. Unfortunately, she'd missed her flight home and the charter group's representative had insisted that she would have to pay full fare for an alternative seat. Miss Millington didn't have the money, so, without regret or recrimination, she had simply answered an advertisement she'd noticed on a placard hung about a young man's neck outside the travel agent's offices. The young man had been the driver of the minibus offering cheap trips to Paris.

Such initiative was all the more remarkable for the fact that it was the first time that Miss Millington has ventured further south than Bognor Regis on the English south coast. She had been on a pilgrimage to the British Forces cemetery at Piraeus, the port just outside the city of Athens. There she had sat quietly beside the grave of Corporal Henry Bevington, her fiancé, who died in action in 1943. Miss Millington had met her young man in 1939, just before the outbreak of the Second World War. She had been a schoolteacher in Cheltenham and Mr Bevington a clerk in a local branch of a national bank. They had both been eager members of a local operatic society. At the outbreak of war Mr Bevington had joined the army and left Miss Millington with a diamond and sapphire ring as a mark of his love and honest intentions. Four years later, all that Miss Millington had left of her fiancé and her future were the ring and a handful of hastily scribbled letters. For nearly half a century she had mourned her loss, taught the ever-arriving and ever-departing young ladies of Cheltenham, visited the theatre in Stratford twice a year and the Opera House in Covent Garden every December.

The young man with the beard and the straggly hair had told Miss Millington that he would take her to Paris where she could catch the express from the Gare du Nord and travel through the Channel Tunnel to England. Within hours of arriving in Paris she could be back home, a few days late but a little wiser and more to talk about for her experience.

0845 hrs. August 4th, Berkshire, England

After she had waved goodbye to her husband, Cynthia Gower

stared thoughtfully at his departing car for a while. She watched it disappear out of the drive and then reappear half a mile away, beginning the slow climb over the chalk downs. She may have seemed innocent and unsuspecting to her husband but she had far less trust in him than he believed. For several months she'd suspected that he had a girlfriend somewhere, probably in London, probably associated with the gallery; and the announcement about her intended visit to a health farm had been nothing more than an invitation designed to encourage her husband to bring his girlfriend out into the open. When she'd watched her husband's car disappear over the brow of the highest ridge on the downs, Cynthia returned inside and telephoned a London number. The receptionist at the detective agency in Sloane Square put her straight through to one of the firm's senior principals.

'He's on his way,' said Cynthia coolly, 'He'll be on the M4 in five or ten minutes.'

'My man's waiting for him. He'll pick him up when he goes onto the slip road.'

'I hope he can keep up with him. My husband has a fast car, a Porsche, and he drives very fast.'

'Don't you worry Mrs Gower,' promised the detective. 'You stay by your telephone and I'll ring you when we have some news.'

0930 hrs. August 4th, rue St Michel, Paris

'The manger won't keep you much longer,' whispered the young woman with the ponytail. She smiled and Cater hesitantly smiled back. When he smiled he looked to be in his early twenties although he was in fact in his late thirties. His boyish haircut helped make him look younger than he was. He looked at his watch when she had turned back to serve her new customer. He had been waiting for nearly three quarters of an hour and his left leg had developed cramp. He shifted carefully and lifted the heavy black plastic case off his knees for a moment.

* * *

Peter Cater was joint managing director of Grammar Press Books and he'd been in Paris for a week collecting orders for books on the new autumn list of the publishing house. The company was still small; apart from Peter and Hugo Turner, his partner, there was just one full time secretary and an editorial assistant, and although they had a share of half a dozen representatives to tour the book shops in the United Kingdom, they still had no representation in Europe. Peter and Hugo had decided to try and sell some of their books in Amsterdam and Paris.

The books they published were ordinary academic volumes, nothing spectacular and nothing designed to worry the best-seller charts. They specialised in the production of books with a certain and steady market, and usually managed to dispose of five hundred books within eighteen months. As a profitable extra side-line they also sold microfilm editions of their own books to major libraries, many of which no longer bought ordinary hard-backed books. Most of the books were on sociological themes but they had also published text books on such varied subjects as agricultural policy, holography and the breaking strains of metals. Their authors were usually highly placed academics who were happy to see their work published without expecting to see any royalties, and who were in a position to recommend to several hundred students that their books be bought. It wasn't exciting or trend-setting publishing but it was moderately profitable.

'He's busy with a customer from the Sorbonne at the moment,' explained the girl with the ponytail. She'd finished with her customer and obviously felt sorry for Peter. 'It's the Assistant Professor in one of the Arts Faculties – I forget which one,' she confided.

'That's all right,' said Cater. He had spent the whole day sitting in bookshops and had sold only twelve volumes of a new treatise on sewage disposal to a shop in Montmartre. And Cater was sure that the bookshop manager had misinterpreted his explanation of the book's contents.

1100 hrs. August 4th, Berkshire, England

She'd fallen asleep in one of the old but comfortable brown leather chairs she kept in the kitchen, and her right arm was temporarily paralysed because of the way she'd been lying. Unable to move for the moment, Cynthia slowly became aware that the telephone was ringing, that it was this which had woken her. She turned her head automatically to look at the kitchen clock and discovered that she'd been asleep for six hours.

'Mrs Gower?'

'Yes,' said Cynthia, rubbing her arm. The feeling was slowly coming back into it but she'd had to pick up the telephone with her left hand.

'Reynolds here,' said the voice at the other end briskly, 'We've got some news for you.'

Cynthia said nothing.

'Are you there?'

'Yes.'

'Is anyone with you?'

'No.'

'Are you all right?'

'I'm fine,' sighed Cynthia, impatiently. 'What's the news?'

'He met a young lady in London. He picked her up at the Hard Rock. It's a café in Piccadilly. Not his usual sort of place, I wouldn't have thought.'

'Where have they gone?'

'He left his car in the underground car park at Hyde Park, and took a taxi to Victoria Station. They had tickets for the Paris train. Our man had a bit of difficulty getting himself a ticket but he managed it. They should be just about there by now.'

'Why the train?' asked Cynthia. 'He doesn't usually go anywhere by train. He always flies.'

'The airlines keep records of European flights,' said the voice from London. 'The railway people just sell the tickets. There's no way of checking up on anyone who crosses the channel by train.'

'Will you ring me when you hear from your man in Paris?'

asked Cynthia. It struck her that the phrase sounded dreadfully melodramatic and for the first time she felt slightly disgusted by the whole business of detectives and errant husbands. She wanted desperately to go away somewhere, find a quiet corner and be alone. But she had to know what was going on, and she wanted her husband back. Somehow, despite his failings, despite his obvious faithlessness, despite his ability to lie to her, she still loved him.

'One of my colleagues will,' promised the man in London. 'I'm going off duty now but there will be someone here in the office all the time.'

'Thank you,' said Cynthia. The feeling was coming back into her arm, and when she'd put the telephone down she rubbed at it vigorously with her free hand.

12.30 hrs. August 4th, Zürich, Switzerland

'Sorry to bother you, Hans, but have you got a moment?'

Bruckner looked up and switched off the dictating machine he'd been using. 'Sit yourself down, Willy, what's troubling you?'

Willy Meier, the marketing director of ACR Drogues et Cie, perched on the corner of Bruckner's enormous – and empty – mahogany desk and leant forward confidentially.

'I think we have a little difficulty with relocating our Angipax production,' said Meier.

'I'll have it sorted within the hour,' promised Bruckner. 'I've found a factory in the English midlands which will be perfect for us. I'm about to call one of the EEC paper pushers. I can get the whole thing sorted out in 48 hours. It'll cost us next to nothing.'

'That is splendid but there's another problem,' said Meier. He spoke wearily, as a man whose life consisted of nothing but problems. 'We're having difficulty moving our raw materials across the channel,' he explained, 'I thought you might be able to help.'

'Transport is not really my area, Willy; what do you think I can do?'

'Well, our transport people tell me that the best and most

efficient and economical way of moving the chemicals across the channel is through the tunnel. We can get the stuff from Paris to Willenhall in less than eight hours. Any other way is going to take longer and be far more expensive.'

Bruckner nodded. 'So what's the problem?'

'The Channel Tunnel Company has a schedule of goods they aren't allowed to carry, mainly for safety reasons. Unfortunately the chemicals we use in the preparation of Angipax are officially regarded as explosives rather than pharmaceuticals. It's a coding problem which is basically a formality, but if we apply to have the schedules changed through the official channels, it'll take months. We need them changed within forty-eight hours.'

Bruckner smiled.

'You see why we need your help?' asked Willy Meier.

'You want me to use a little muscle and get it sorted out?'

'Well, you've got the connections, Hans.'

'OK,' said Bruckner. 'Give me all the details and I'll do what I can.'

12.37 hrs. August 4th, St. Malo, Brittany

Mrs Black put down the fish slice she was holding and pulled at the caravan cupboard with both hands. The wood had swollen with the dampness and once again the cupboard door had jammed.

'Will someone come and help me with this cupboard?' she called, tugging furiously at the cupboard's cream plastic handle. She was slight and small, although in recent years a spread of comfortable fat had begun to settle around her hips. Beside her husband, a huge fifteen stone man with thinning ginger hair and a pale unhealthy complexion, she looked radiantly healthy and shapely.

Her husband, David, was deep in a paperback book on the front cover of which a semi-naked blonde nurse could be seen attempting to elude the clutches of a man in a pair of bright red pyjamas. He took no notice of his wife's appeal. James Black, and Louise Black, aged 16 and 14 years respectively, were busy arguing over which station to listen to on the portable radio set which stood on the caravan table. They too ignored their mother's cry for help.

Suddenly the cupboard door flew open and Mrs Black shot backwards against the tiny sink a couple of feet behind her.

'Now look what's happened!' she screamed, as the contents of the cupboard tumbled out onto the stove below. A packet of salt and a plastic bottle of tomato ketchup fell into the frying pan in which half a dozen rashers of bacon were lying ready for the stove to be lit. The small avalanche also sent a packet of plastic forks flying onto the floor.

'Don't make so much fuss, dear,' said Mr Black, without looking up from his book.

'Mum, I want to listen to Radio London,' said Louise. 'And Jimmy wants to listen to that French station.'

'Look at this mess,' moaned Mrs Black.

'We had this programme on all day yesterday,' complained Louise.

'Well, what's the point of coming over here if we spend all the time listening to that rubbishy pirate station?' demanded James. 'We can listen to that all day at home.'

'The salt packet's split,' said Mrs Black. 'And there's salt everywhere.'

'I wish you lot would shut up,' shouted Mr Black, 'We're supposed to be on holiday. Louise, help your mother. And put that damned radio off. If you can't decide what you want to listen to, we'll have a little peace and quiet.'

'That's not fair,' said Louise, 'I helped all day yesterday'.

'Do as your father says,' said Mrs Black.

'I'm fed up with this holiday,' muttered Louise.

'We're not having bacon again, are we?' asked James, taking an interest in the frying pan for the first time. 'We've eaten nothing but bacon for days. I think I'm going to become a vegetarian.'

'Bloody hell!' screamed Mr Black, banging his book down again and sending four plastic knives and a stack of paper plates to the floor, where they joined the plastic forks. 'I've just about had enough of you pair. It's not my fault it's been raining for the last ten days. It's not my bloody fault if the camp shop sells nothing but stuff we either can't eat or can't afford, and it's not my bloody fault the cupboard door keeps sticking.'

'No one said it was, dear,' said Mrs Black, attempting to calm her irate husband. 'Now do calm down. You know what the doctor said.'

'Everyone seems to think it is,' roared Mr Black unfairly. 'And I'm not having another week of it.'

'No, dear,' said Mrs Black. 'I'm sure the children didn't mean to upset you.'

'We're going back when you've finished burning that bacon,' said Mr Black.

'We can't go back,' said Mrs Black. 'We aren't booked to go back for another week.'

The last few words of Mrs Black's sentence were drowned by the sound of thunder breaking. Seconds later the caravan roof was hit by the first few thousand drops of a storm that was to last for the next twelve hours and to cover north-western France. For the Blacks it was the final straw. They had spent three weeks touring France and for ten of those twenty-one days it had rained. Living in a tiny caravan is never easy; when the occupants have little in common other than family ties, the greatest possible co-operation from the weather is required.

An hour and a half after they had finished their meal, the Black family set off for Paris.

12.55 hrs. August 4th, Bd. De Sébastopol, Paris

Outside the shop, two elderly men were standing studying the contents of the window. In all there must have been nearly two hundred magazines on display and on every one of them there was a coloured photograph of one or more naked human bodies.

There were photographs of women and men, women and women, and men and men. There were photographs of women with enormous breasts, women with neat round breasts and women with huge plastic dildos strapped to their bodies; and there were photographs that were to the casual observer quite incomprehensible.

Inside the shop Peter Cater was standing impatiently waiting for the proprietor to finish serving a customer. The two young girls who normally attended to customers were away at lunch.

'What have you got for me this time?' asked Luillard when he'd led Cater through into the office which lay behind the shop. He took a bottle of Pernod down from the mantelpiece and poured two generous drinks. A stoppered bottle of water already sat on the table.

'I've got some more photographs of Felicity,' said Peter. 'Two rolls.' He took the camera from around his neck and opened the back. Inside there was not one but two rolls of film, both fully exposed and fitting neatly into the available space which had been adapted specially for this purpose. Cater had been smuggling pornographic photographs across the channel for two years in this simple but effective way.

'Marvellous!' said Luillard, taking the films from Peter enthusiastically. Felicity Henshaw was a young woman of twenty-five who looked like a girl of sixteen, thanks to natural inadequacies in her hormonal make up. Peter Cater had taken several hundred photographs of her in carefully posed situations with a series of well-built male models.

The two men studied the negatives in Luillard's darkroom; the workshop where many of the magazines displayed in the shop window had been created and the hub of his growing publishing empire. They said little although occasionally Luillard gave out a grunt of professional satisfaction.

Twenty minutes later Cater carefully pocketed the ten five-hundred franc notes that Luillard had given him and left the shop. The two old men were still studying the window display and the two girls had not yet returned from lunch. As he walked away Cater wondered, as he always did, what his wife and partner would say if they knew about his additional business activities. As always, he told himself that it was only until he had enough money to set up a proper publishing house of his own. Or, better still, to retire to the country and write the novel he was desperate to start.

12.59 hrs. August 4th, Zürich, Switzerland

When Meier had gone, and he'd finished the dictation which had been interrupted, Bruckner pulled on his fur-collared overcoat, told his secretary he'd be out for a few moments, and picked up his Bentley from the executives' garage in the basement of the drug company's building. He waved aside the duty chauffeur who stepped forward as soon as he appeared in the garage.

Apart from a villa on the south side or the Zürichersee, he had a luxury apartment in the centre of the town. Parking the car in the underground garage at the apartment block, he took the lift to the sixth floor. Bruckner's apartment occupied one half of the entire floor and was as well guarded by security systems as most bank vaults. A special walk-in safe had been installed in the apartment, and it was so well built that even if the entire block had collapsed the safe would have remained unscathed. It was to the safe that Bruckner went as soon as he had secured the front door.

Inside the safe, Bruckner kept dossiers on all major politicians. Naturally the thickest files concerned EEC politicians, but there were also files on leading figures in all the world's political parties. It was these files which gave Bruckner his enormous commercial strength, and since he had built them up at his own expense during fifteen years of rising from a minor management post in a small Swiss bank Bruckner kept the files at his own home rather than at his office. Too many of his contemporaries had found themselves fired by their employers and had found their offices locked and sealed within minutes of receiving their dismissal notices. Bruckner wasn't taking any chances with his private files.

With the development of national and international bureaucratic institutions in the sixties and seventies, Bruckner had discovered that his information files, which were kept scrupulously up-to-date with the aid of a number of well-paid informants throughout the world, gave him a considerable amount of power over these institutions. Civil servants and official employees may sometimes be honest and reliable but politicians, because of their very natures, are often guilty of indiscretions and susceptible to bribery. And, of course, in any democracy it is the politicians who have the ultimate authority over public or commercial administrations.

Bruckner's file on the current French Transport Minister was slim but adequate. His files on the members of the board of the Compagnie de Chemin de Fer Sous-marin Entre La France et L'Angleterre were even more satisfactory. After studying them for no more than a few moments and making notes in a small black leather loose-leaf notebook in a private shorthand, Bruckner replaced the files in their cabinets, sealed the vault and returned to the ACR Drogues et Cie building. He had been away for just under three-quarters of an hour and he had other things to attend to.

14.32 hrs. August 4th, Luxembourg

Susan Roberts closed the file on her desk with a snap and tossed it angrily into the tray on her right.

She picked up a second file and opened it. This one, like the first, concerned financial aspects of the European car industry. Miss Roberts, whose prim and precise appearance and manner reminded many of a spinster schoolteacher or rather proper woman newsreader, looked like a superior private secretary, but in fact she was an assistant secretary-general of the European Credit Bank, a central loan source for the European Economic Community. She was responsible for ensuring that loans made to companies in member states were both economically sound and industrially wise. Her neatly curled hair, pair of old-fashioned pendulous earrings, and thin row of pearls, provided Miss Roberts with a wonderful protective disguise. She looked harmless and innocent, whereas in fact she was neither.

The EEC secretariat was becoming publicly sceptical about some of the loans made by the bank in recent years. Some, they claimed, were unlikely to be repaid, since the organisations which had received them were on the verge of collapse. In other areas, they went on, companies were not receiving vital aid, and as a direct consequence were failing. The failure of these companies left the EEC Secretariat with the job of providing redundancy payments and unemployment pay. The Permanent Under-Secretary of the Treasury in Brussels had made a number of scathing comments about the inability of the Credit Bank to put its money on the right horses.

Miss Roberts had, several months previously, promised to give a permanently ailing part of the British car industry £250 million as a short term loan to aid in the production of a new model. A fifth of the allocation had already been spent on pursuing and levelling a factory site in the West Midlands and on building a factory shell. Now the company had been refused a grant previously promised by the British Government and there seemed every likelihood that the company would finally go to the wall. There were six thousand jobs at stake and there seemed every possibility that the £250 million would take years to recover. At best it would be recovered without interest.

Throwing down the second file with a sigh, Miss Roberts left her desk and walked across the room to a door on her left. The door led into a small room, no more than six feet square, that contained a sunken bath and a complicated-looking panel of switches and controls. Slipping out of her clothes Miss Roberts strapped waterproof leads to her wrists and ankles. Her body was well-kept if slightly curvaceous for current tastes.

She then pressed a chromium-plated button in the wall above the bath and turned a small dial just underneath it. The bath filled rapidly with water at the selected temperature. The thermostat would keep the water in the bath at that temperature, letting cooling water out and replacing it with warmer water. The changing of the water was pleasantly refreshing and ensured that the water remained fresh and clean. There was even a device which enabled those so inclined to keep their bath water supplied with bath salts and fragrances.

Lying in the bath Miss Roberts could look straight at a screen upon which three graphs were clearly visible. The topmost graph represented her blood pressure, the middle one her pulse rate, and the lower one the muscle tension in her arms and legs. The lines were red but as she relaxed they would gradually turn first yellow and then green.

Rested and relaxed forty minutes later, Miss Roberts reached up to speak to her personal secretary on the intercom. He had news about an important telephone call from Zürich. The finance director of ACR Drogues et Cie, a major Swiss pharmaceutical company, had rung twice in the last thirty minutes. His company had an urgent proposal to make which they thought might interest the Bank.

'Shall I ring him back?' demanded Gaston Raenackers, her secretary.

'I'll speak to him here.'

Seconds later Herr Bruckner in Zürich was talking to Miss Roberts in her bath in Luxembourg; she was grateful that she hadn't had a visiphone installed in the bathroom despite the appeals of the decorator who'd designed her office suite. She couldn't see Swiss finance directors taking kindly to discussions of such an informal nature. The Swiss were always so very, very proper, particularly when it came to talking about money.

'I think we may be able to help each other,' began Bruckner. 'We are looking for a factory site in England and the agents we usually deal with tell us there is a property in Willenhall which we might be able to get hold of.'

'You need somewhere urgently?' asked Miss Roberts cautiously.

'A new project of ours,' said Bruckner. 'It's proved so successful that we cannot cope with the demand. We're looking for a factory site and warehouse space, preferably somewhere in the Midlands.'

'Do you have anywhere particular in mind?'

'You know very well what I'm talking about, my dear,' said Bruckner. 'You have £250 million tied up in Willenhall. We'll bail you out if you can speed things up for us.'

'Why the hurry?' asked Miss Roberts, ever suspicious.

'We had a fire in our major French warehouse yesterday,' explained Bruckner. 'It couldn't have come at a worse time; just as we're promoting a new product. We have a good supply of the raw materials we use for the drug, and the preparation of the product is a relatively simple if technologically advanced technique. It will be quicker and more efficient for us to continue half our manufacturing in Britain.'

'What's the deal?' asked Miss Roberts, who always liked to think of herself as a dealmaker rather than as the bureaucrat she was. The lines on the screen above her had turned back to yellow.

'We'll take over the entire property in Willenhall,' said Bruckner. 'The car people haven't moved in yet; we can move machinery into it before the end of the week.'

'And you'll take over the loan?' suggested Miss Roberts.

'That's right,' said Bruckner. 'I'm not pretending it isn't a good deal for us. But it gets you out of a hole.'

'So how do you want to arrange it?' asked Miss Roberts. The lines on the screen had turned red.

'Can you be in England tomorrow?' asked Bruckner. 'The English won't budge out of London. We can fix everything up there.'

'OK,' agreed Miss Roberts. 'I can manage that.'

'I'll fix it up with Kennan, the chap at the English end,' promised Bruckner. 'We'll meet you at the ACR offices in Leicester Square if that's all right with you?'

'Fine,' said Miss Roberts. The ACR offices were known for their opulence and for the fine wines and food always served to visitors. Visiting bankers and politicians were always delighted by an invitation. She heard a click as Bruckner severed the connection and then lay back for a few moments and enjoyed the warmth of the water. She watched the lines of the screen turn yellow as she deliberately relaxed her body again.

'Have you finished?' asked Raenackers, through the intercom.

'Yes, thank you, Gaston,' said Miss Roberts. 'I think we've sorted out that damned Willenhall project.'

'That's marvellous, Miss Roberts,' said Gaston, sounding genuinely pleased.

'Bring the cognac in, Gaston, I think we can celebrate,' said the Assistant Secretary-General. 'And bring two glasses.' She turned off the intercom and lay back.

* * *

Gaston Raenackers had worked for Miss Roberts as her assistant for eighteen months. In his early and mid-twenties, he had studied in Brussels at the Centre for International Business Studies where in addition to accountancy and taxation he had studied shorthand and typing. He had also taken a special course in EEC Regulations, which had given him a solid basic understanding of the rules which governed trading between member states of the community. At the age of 27, he had obtained a job with the international division of Barclay's Bank as a clerk in the Securities Department at the Brussels branch. While working there, he met Miss Roberts, who had been in Brussels at a conference organised by the bank.

On the first afternoon, while Raenacker's senior had been speaking, Miss Roberts and he had discovered a certain raw sexual compatibility. Susan Roberts preferred to play a dominant role in her sexual encounters while Raenackers enjoyed a more passive role. His tendency to ejaculate only after continued and heavy sexual exercise was for Miss Roberts a heaven-sent advantage. A week after returning to the American Bank's headquarters in Geneva she sacked her personal assistant, a sad-faced blonde girl with an unlikely chest, and Raenackers joined her there at the end of the month. When Miss Roberts moved to the European Credit Bank in Luxembourg, Raenackers moved with her.

There was therefore, no need for Raenackers to say anything when he entered the small steamy relaxation room where Miss Roberts lay soaking and naked. Nor was there any need for her to say anything. Raenackers first poured two large brandies and then slowly and provocatively undressed.

The lines on the screen above the bath were glowing bright red when Miss Roberts removed the leads from her wrists and ankles. Slipping off his black silk G-string, Raenackers lay flat on his back on the carpet. He sipped at his brandy, holding himself up on one elbow, as his employer climbed out of the bath and, still dripping wet, lowered herself onto him. As ever, he was fully distended and Miss Roberts was well satisfied.

1705 hrs. August 4th, rue Réaumur, Paris

For years the rue Réaumur has been the centre in Paris for

numismatists. Squeezed in between the big newspaper and magazine offices there are many small shops selling and buying coins. A few minutes after leaving the publisher's office, Cater walked into one of the newest of the shops. There he bought two fine examples of silver Roman coinage. Together the two coins cost several thousand francs; just slightly less than the sum that he had received from the publisher.

Outside the shop Cater hurried away. He stopped at a café nearby and walked straight into a toilet cubicle. There he thoughtfully examined the two coins before slipping them into his jacket pocket. He took care to put them into a pocket which contained no other coins and in which an empty envelope apparently fortuitously separated the coins. The two red plastic boxes from which he had taken the coins he pushed to the bottom of a bulging black plastic waste-bag in a corner of the cubicle.

Then he went to a table at the back of the café and ordered a croque monsieur and an espresso coffee.

1717 hrs. August 4th, Zürich, Switzerland

Like most Swiss, Bruckner was meticulously polite and always careful to avoid giving gratuitous offence. When telephoning the French Transport Minister, he dialled the number himself to ensure that there was no chance of the Minister being allowed to pick up a telephone and find himself waiting for Bruckner to come onto the line. He dialled the private number at the Minister's office that he'd taken from his file, and spoke to the Minister's personal secretary, who gave him the number of a restaurant just off the place Vendôme where the Minister was dining with friends. Bruckner smiled to himself when the secretary told him that. He knew all about the Minister's friends and had he been less far-sighted he could have sold the information to any of the major news magazines for a few thousand francs. It wouldn't have been the first time that Bruckner had recouped some of his expenses that way.

'Good afternoon,' snapped the Minister. 'I hope this is urgent.' He sounded half-drunk, and Bruckner hoped that the fool was sober enough to know what was happening.

'It is, Minister. I think you'll agree with me that it is,' he murmured quietly. 'We haven't met but my name is Bruckner. I'm calling from Zürich.'

More than once, simply by giving his name had been enough. Gossip about his private filing system had given Bruckner a considerable reputation in Europe. Bruckner didn't object at all; if anything, it made each problem simpler than the one before. He had only to ruin three or four well-established politicians to acquire a reputation for straight dealing and for being a man of his word. Even if some of the words were perhaps rather menacing.

The French Minister, however, either hadn't heard of Bruckner or else he was too drunk to think clearly. He merely repeated his initial greeting. In the background Bruckner heard someone laugh. It sounded like a young girl but could have been a young man.

'I'm ringing on behalf of my employers, ACR Drogues from Zürich,' said Bruckner. 'I was rather hoping that we might be able to persuade you to help us with a transport problem.'

'You're not getting off to a very good start by ringing me here,' said the Minister tartly. 'Ring me at my office at about eleven tomorrow.'

'I'm afraid it's rather urgent,' said Bruckner. 'And we do have a mutual financial interest.'

The reference to money caught the Minister's attention. He didn't hang up.

'A young friend of yours called Tony Kitchen, is now working for us,' said Bruckner quietly. 'And quite frankly he's a dreadful problem to us.' Bruckner could hear the Minister's respiratory rate increase.

'What about him?' snapped the Minister.

'He wants another pay rise and we really can't afford to give him one,' explained Bruckner. 'But he did say that you and he were old friends and that for his sake you might do us a small favour.'

'What are you talking about?' The demand was cold and quick but Bruckner sensed a change in the man's attitude. He sounded less arrogant, less sure of himself.

'If you could help us we'd obviously be pleased with him and be able to give him what he wants. Then we'd all be happy, wouldn't we?' said Bruckner slowly. He wanted his man to be well and truly on the line.

'I know what you're saying,' said the Minister. 'What do you want?'

Bruckner explained, speaking slowly and carefully.

'A courier will be with you in a few hours' time with a packet containing details of the schedules of acceptable cargo for the tunnel train. There's a purely technical point which is likely to prove an embarrassing problem for us unless we can get your help,' explained Bruckner. 'All I want you to do is to pass the revised schedule and make one telephone call.'

'I can't change schedules like that,' said the Minister. 'It can't be done.'

'Oh, I'm sure it can,' said Bruckner softly but with menace. 'Stay where you are and in thirty minutes I'll ring you back with a name and a telephone number. All you have to do is to ring the number I give you and tell the man at the other end that you've approved some new schedules and that you want the Channel Tunnel Company board to approve them as well.'

There was a pause.

'What about Kitchen?'

'I don't think there will be any need for you to worry about him,' said Bruckner. 'I'll ring back in thirty minutes.' He put the telephone down and waited for a moment before dialling a second number, this time in Athens.

* * *

The telephone system in Greece wasn't as efficient as the one in Switzerland and, despite the courtesy and willingness of the operator at the Grande Bretagne Hotel, Bruckner had to dial three times before he got a decent line. Luckily, Robert Merlin was in his room and Bruckner was able to get straight through to him without any further delay.

'I believe there's a meeting of the Channel Tunnel Company board tomorrow,' said Bruckner after introducing himself.

'There is,' agreed Merlin. 'But I shan't be going.'

'That's a great pity,' said Bruckner, with obvious

disappointment. 'I was hoping that we could do some mutually advantageous business together.'

Merlin, who knew Bruckner's reputation, waited.

'We're having a little difficulty in moving some pharmaceuticals across the channel,' Bruckner explained. He told Merlin the problem and pointed out that the Minister had already passed the revised schedule.

'There won't be any chance to bring this up tomorrow,' said Merlin.

'You could bring it up under 'any other business',' Bruckner pointed out.

'I could, I suppose,' said Merlin. 'But I'm not going to the meeting.'

'That's a tremendous pity for both of us,' said Bruckner.

'Why?' Merlin found Bruckner's calm approach inexplicably worrying.

'I believe you have a personal account with the Berne International Bank,' said Bruckner.

'What of it?'

'You have a loan facility approaching half a million Swiss francs.'

'How do you know what private arrangements I have with my bank?'

'And the bank has an immediate recall on the loan?'

'Are you threatening me?'

'Of course not. But your bank happens to be one of our leading shareholders. They would lose money if the marketing programme for our new drug didn't do well. If they lost money they would undoubtedly feel a need to call in some of their loans. Unfortunately, it is the way...'

'You want me to get the board to pass the new schedule?' asked Merlin after a pause.

'It won't be a problem for you,' promised Bruckner. 'You will have a letter from the Minister of Transport, and the chairman will be Noiret. He will approve the plan if it has got the Minister's approval. Particularly if he knows nothing about it beforehand. Noiret is paranoid and he'll be convinced that there's something going on behind his back; something that maybe threatens his position. He won't do anything rash until he knows what is going on.'

'You know a lot about everyone,' said Merlin.

'That's my job.'

The rest of it was easy. Another telephone call to the Minister. A package for a courier to take to Paris. Arrangements for a private jet to pick up Merlin from Athens airport, and finally a telephone call to Meier.

'You can get your people to have the chemicals ready for the tunnel train tomorrow.'

Willy Meier thanked the gods, not for the first time, that he was on the same side as Bruckner.

2335 hrs. August 4th, Montmartre, Paris

During the hours of daylight, the boulevard de Clichy looks dull, grey and unexciting. It looks the sort of wide Parisian street where importers and exporters, dealers of all kinds and unsuccessful insurance brokers have their offices.

At night, however, during the hours of darkness, the boulevard de Clichy changes beyond all recognition. It blossoms like a garden that has been hiding its colours and movement away from the cold of the winter. The shutters are pulled back or taken down and the doorways are unbolted. The windows are filled with brightly-lit colour photographs of Parisian ladies dressed in the traditional costume of the district; a few pieces of black silk edged with red lace. The doorways are occupied by men in evening suits lounging lazily with one shoulder against the doorframe. And suddenly you are aware that the buildings you thought were deserted are decorated on the outside with neon lights and illuminated pictures. The boulevard de Clichy can no longer be described as dull, grey or unexciting. It is, as it has been for several decades, the centre of a certain type of Parisian nightlife.

Moving past a pair of streetwalkers arguing vociferously and threatening violence to each other, Alan Cannon looked at his watch. It was twenty minutes to one. No wonder the pedestrians, both clients and suppliers, were beginning to look weary and more than a little drunk. Even though the wine, whisky and champagne sold was largely watered, enough of it had been drunk to erase the normal niceties from the social behaviour of most of the district's visitors and inhabitants. It was about time, decided Cannon, that he found what he'd come looking for.

* * *

Alan Cannon, plump, of medium height and almost completely bald, was the European Manager of an American Company called Georges Investment Corporation, which specialised in the manufacture and installation of small home computers. These enabled householders to deal with all bills, all repair problems, all investments and insurance policies, and all other personal matters such as taxation and the buying of food, furniture and energy supplies through a single agency. The home computers which GIC sold were linked by telephone to a series of computer centres, each only the size of an ordinary shop but capable of dealing with information from a quarter of a million homes. When a customer of GIC bought his computer, he also signed an agreement to subscribe annually for the rest of his life to a special GIC Householder Service. By making the cost of the computer ridiculously small, and the cost of the monthly payments to the service apparently small, GIC had managed to obtain 30 million customers in Europe in the space of three years. The company claimed to be growing faster than any other company in the world. All a customer had to do when he had bought his computer was tap onto the keyboard information about his regular commitments, and then allow the computer to manage his affairs. Requests for special supplies and for repairs to be dealt with were fed into the computer in exactly the same way. Orders were then passed on to local shops and repair agencies, which received their instructions direct from the nearest computer centre. If necessary the computer would even arrange hire purchase or a loan.

Alan Cannon lived and worked in London and controlled the entire European operation. There were 180 computer centres installed in eight different European countries, and each of them was run by a manger who operated with no more than one or perhaps two assistants. When the manager was ill, or away on holiday, a replacement would be flown in. Cannon had a team of twenty-five travelling replacement managers permanently available. At any one time about twenty of them would be working while the others waited on stand-by. Cannon himself was seemingly full of energy; he never seemed to switch off and relax.

While outside a sex shop in the rue des Martyrs, which sold the usual variety of sex aids, inflatable blondes and vibrating plastic penises, and also served as the foyer to a club which boasted activities which even the raunchiest centres of Amsterdam's red light district would have been shy to publicise, Cannon was approached by a woman in her late fifties. The make-up she wore disguised that fact to a certain extent.

As Cannon walked past her she called huskily to him, and when he turned in her direction she pulled surreptitiously at her blouse, revealing a good two thirds of her chest. She looked as if she'd been decorated and made up by some whimsical artist determined to recreate a classical model of the traditional French prostitute. Fishnet stockings, a red handbag, a split, tight skirt and a black silk blouse trimmed with flimsy lace covered those parts of her not painted with lipstick, eyeshadow and face powder. The cleft between her breasts, deep enough in itself, had been accentuated by a flash of crudely applied red lipstick.

Cannon followed her up scruffy wooden stairs which they reached through an unmarked wooden door on the right of the sex shop. As they climbed, Cannon found it impossible to take his eyes off the woman's swaying behind. At the top of the stairs the woman paused, wheezing, and turned round to make sure that Cannon was following her. In the harsh light of a single unshaded bulb Cannon could for the first time see what he was hiring but strangely he felt a flood of sexual tension as he stared at this hideously painted creature. She turned quickly to the right, walked half a dozen paces down a dingy corridor, which became more and more dimly lit as they moved away from the single naked bulb, and stopped outside a brown painted door on which was painted in small white letters the single name Anne.

The room was no more than eight feet square and contained

nothing more than a bed and a small wooden chair. Behind the door a coathanger rattled against the wood as the woman pushed to ensure that the door catch had caught. Having ensured that the door was locked, the woman, who had turned on the room's only light, a small red bulb in a lamp hanging over the bed, moved towards Cannon in which she clearly intended to be a sensual way. Cannon felt himself filling with desire for this woman. Skilfully she unbuttoned her blouse and released her breasts from their harness. Cannon undressed too. The woman looked older now. She was wheezing and looking pale, as though the short walk had worn her out.

Suddenly, as if remembering something she'd forgotten, the woman held out one hand, palm upwards. She rubbed the thumb against the base of her fingers.

'Cent,' she muttered. 'Cent francs.'

It was more than she usually made and Cannon knew it but he turned round and reached for his bill clip in his trouser pocket. He took a hundred-franc note from it and handed it to the woman who with a smile tucked it under the pillow.

Pulling Cannon with her the woman lay down on top of the bed. As he moved between her legs she lifted her knees and wrapped her calves around his back. Her lips parted and she opened her eyes wide in mock expectation. Cannon manoeuvred gently into position and thrust forwards, taking her breasts in his hands and squeezing them tightly until the woman grimaced. When her mouth opened wider – with pain, not an affectation of lust – Cannon moved one hand and placed it firmly across her lips. He felt her top set of false teeth slip under the force of his palm. He pushed harder and more fiercely against her and felt her body begin to writhe with what he thought was a mixture of genuine pleasure and unexpected pain. Lifting his hand he lowered his head and pushed his lips against hers. Behind his back her ankles pulled tightly. He pushed into her harder, moving faster and faster. For a moment or two she moved with him.

Suddenly, inexplicably, Cannon felt her pull away from him, felt the tension of her muscles behind his back weaken, felt her lips lose their urgency. He pushed harder and returned both hands to her breasts, feeling for her nipples with his fingers. She gasped for breath and started feebly to fight him. The flailing arms suddenly stopped moving. He pushed again. This time she did not react. Feeling cold, and knowing suddenly that his erection had been extinguished even more quickly than it had appeared, Cannon pulled away. He felt her ankles slide across his back and land with a thump on the bed.

Scrambling to the side of the bed Cannon reached for the floor with his feet. It felt greasy and gritty. He instinctively stood on tip toe and turned around looking for his socks. Having found them he turned back to the woman on the bed. He knew without touching her that she was dead. Beneath the rouge on her cheeks and the lipstick smear between her breasts she looked white. Cannon dressed quickly and silently. He couldn't look back at the bed but, as quietly as he could, opened the door and stepped out into the corridor. It was as deserted as it had been when they'd arrived. Less than a minute later he was in the street, walking away from the doorway and the sex shop with his head hanging low. He shivered and could feel the sweat dripping off the tip of his nose as he walked. She must have had a heart attack. It was hardly surprising. She hadn't looked the sort of woman to watch her diet or look after herself. But would the police believe him? They might have been convinced that he'd killed her. Would he be able to prove that he hadn't? Even if he could, the publicity would hardly help his career. The American board of the company were very strict, almost puritanical. They preferred comfortably married men. They wouldn't be pleased to hear about their European manager screwing middle-aged hookers in Montmartre. Even if he could prove he hadn't murdered her. Even if he hadn't murdered her. Had he? He couldn't remember. Sweating, he just walked on, heading without knowledge or firm intention for anywhere away from the rue des Martyrs.

* * *

For two hours after leaving the small room in the rue des Martyrs Alan Cannon wandered around Montmartre in a daze. At three in the morning, with the streets quiet at last and the shop windows abandoned by their tenants, he stopped at an all-night café in the rue d'Amsterdam. He sat with a half litre of red wine and a basket full of steaming hot croissants trying to avoid the eye of a girl with shorn red hair who looked hardly into her 'teens and whose business ambitions were clearly simple and traditional.

From there he'd gone into the Gare St Lazare, where he'd wandered around aimlessly until a patrolling gendarme seemed to take an interest in him. Then he'd bought a ticket from one of the automatic ticket dispensers in the concourse and caught a train to Versailles. At Versailles he'd bought a return ticket after hanging around outside the station for ten minutes. He'd arrived back in Paris at half past five.

The next four hours seemed like a lifetime. Twenty times he emptied his pockets and tried to decide if he'd lost anything; left anything in the room with the dead woman. He examined his wallet, comb, keys, cheque book, pen, notebook, passport, identification papers, handkerchief. Everything seemed to be there. But had he left a book of matches there? Had he left fingerprints? Could the police identify him from his semen? He couldn't even remember whether or not he had ejaculated.

All he could think of was the woman's cold grey face, her mouth slightly open, her eyes staring up at the ceiling, her legs slightly apart and bent at the knees. And her varicose veins, marked out as if with a blue pencil.

Eventually, as the station clock reached half-past nine and the last of the morning commuters filed away from the station, Cannon decided that he had to go back to the hotel. He had to collect his bag and check out of the hotel. He decided not to take a taxi and not to even risk a ride on the Metro. He would walk. Turn right outside the station, straight along the rue de la Pepinière, across the place St Augustin, along the rue la Boëtie and straight across the Avenue des Champs Elysées into the rue Pierre Charron. Here the people wake later and the early morning activity was slight. From the end of the rue Pierre Charron, Alan Cannon could see the Hotel George V. It looked formidable and disapproving.

The doorman touched his hat as Cannon approached. Cannon gave thanks to his supervising angel that he had booked in at an exclusive hotel where the staff make no public note of the eccentricities of the patrons. Walking straight through the hotel lobby Cannon went straight into the dining room. Most of the guests had breakfasted and Canon sat alone in a far corner of the restaurant to eat his meal. After two cups of coffee and two soft rolls he headed for his room.

The newspaper he'd ordered was on his bedside table. Despite the fact that it was an English evening paper and twelve hours out of date, Cannon searched it for any reference to the woman of the rue des Martyrs. He'd searched the *International Herald Tribune*, too, with equal lack of success. Hardly surprising, since both papers had been composed and printed hours before he'd met the woman.

At eleven thirty, still with no idea about what to do next Cannon checked out of the hotel, paying his bill with cash.

'Are you leaving already?' asked the desk clerk, as Cannon paid his bill.

Cannon nodded.

'Going back to England?' asked the clerk.

'Yes,' said Cannon. Couldn't the man mind his own business?

'Have a good flight,' smiled the clerk.

'Thank you,' said Cannon, accepting his change from the cashier. It was then that he decided to go home not by air, but by train. At two o'clock he boarded the train to Sangatte with a ticket for the tunnel train in his pocket.

PART TWO

0700 hrs. August 5th, Sangatte

Susan Roberts and Gaston Raenackers left Luxembourg on the evening of the 4th August. It was 8.00 pm when they arrived at Sangatte and took a taxi to the Terminal Hotel. Raenackers had arranged their tickets for the following day's train at 6.20 pm. He had also booked two adjoining rooms in the hotel. For Miss Roberts there was a suite, consisting of a bedroom, bathroom and sitting room. For Raenackers a bedroom and bathroom. As a senior official of the European Credit Bank, Miss Roberts was always careful to ensure that her behaviour was beyond reproach. Too often in the past, senior officials had been pilloried by the popular press for their personal tastes and preferences in entertainment and amusement.

They dined separately and by ten were both comfortably ensconced in their respective bedrooms. Raenackers telephoned the manager's office and left instructions that they were not to be disturbed until further notice, giving as an excuse the fact that they had been both engaged in long-lasting negotiations in Luxembourg over the previous forty-eight hours. As an additional precaution they both hung 'Do Not Disturb' notices on their door handles. After making his telephone call, however, Raenackers left his room, made sure that the corridor was deserted, and was admitted to the suite occupied by Miss Roberts.

0715 hrs. August 5th, St Quentin

Shortly after dawn on the 5th August, two huge containers were taken from the ACR Drogues factory at St Quentin en Yvelines to the nearest container depot twelve kilometres away. The containers, one loaded with erythrytyl tetranitrate and the other with pentaerythritol tetranitrate, were sealed at the factory by two inspectors from the Union Internationale des Transports Combinés Rail/Route and the Office of the Council of Transport Ministers. The two inspectors, who were given the authority to inspect and either allow or delay the passage of goods, had the responsibility of ensuring that the goods being loaded into the containers were filled with what they were claimed to contain. Once the necessary seals had been affixed and the requisite papers stamped and signed, the two containers could be transported across any frontiers within the Common Market without being opened or being checked again. The system had been introduced to reduce delays to freight moving about within member countries and it worked extremely well.

0800 hrs. August 5th, Hotel Continental, Paris

'Marvellous dinner last night,' said Dr Chatwyn, pouring himself a third cup of black coffee and waving towards an empty chair as his colleague approached.

'Tremendous,' agreed Dr Singh heartily, sitting himself down and picking up the breakfast menu. A neighbouring waiter sauntered over lazily. It was nearly half-past ten and the dining room was due to close in a few moments' time. The waiter fussed around, flicking bread crumbs from the table cloth, hoping that the dining room clock would hurry up, so that he could refuse the latecomer anything more than coffee and what toast was already on the table.

'Just coffee, please, said Singh, taking a piece of toast from the rack in front of Chatwyn.

'Did us well, those boys from ACR,' said Chatwyn, motioning to the waiter to bring more toast with the fresh coffee.

'Are you sure you don't want to fly?' asked Singh. 'I checked with the agency at the hotel reception desk. They can fit us on a flight at four-thirty.'

'I can't stand aeroplanes,' said Chatwyn. 'The train is the only civilised way to travel these days.'

'What time is the train?' asked Singh.

'Two,' replied Chatwyn, 'It gets us into London about eight tonight.'

'I needed that,' said Singh, swallowing half a cup of coffee in a single gulp. 'I had far too much to drink last night.'

'What did you think of the stuff they were promoting?' asked Chatwyn.

'They've got some pretty impressive evidence about its effectiveness,' Singh replied. 'You think how many men in their thirties, forties, fifties and sixties are getting angina in Europe alone.'

'And the women,' Chatwyn reminded him. 'Angina is getting more and more common in women, too.'

'With all those people taking four tablets of Angipax a day to keep their angina under control, they'll be able to afford to push the boat out for a few doctors occasionally!'

* * *

Dr Chatwyn had never intended to become a doctor. He had drifted to medical school on a wave of artificial enthusiasm whipped up by his parents and schoolteachers who were all impressed by his academic skills. In the upper forms of his comprehensive school he had been the only pupil with more than average academic expectations and his ambitions had been moulded for him. At medical school he had no longer been an intellectual man among boys; his contemporaries there had equal academic skills. But they had something else: they had confidence.

It would not have been so bad if his academic success had continued. At least, then, Chatwyn might perhaps have managed to acquire a little confidence of his own. Unfortunately, despite the fact that he spent every available minute poring over textbooks, studying microscope slides and examining specimens in the various museums Chatwyn simply managed to keep up with the mainstream of students. Back home his parents and teachers waited anxiously for news of their protégé's success. They expected to hear of scholarships and prizes, distinctions and awards. Nothing came. Chatwyn stayed at the medical school during holidays to concentrate on his book work but could achieve nothing remotely resembling academic success. His parents had difficulty in hiding their disappointment.

Somehow Chatwyn managed to qualify. His colleagues disappeared into local hospitals to do their house jobs and register themselves with the General Medical Council. Desperately Chatwyn studied the list of jobs available. By a stroke of fortune he discovered that the Department of Pharmacology had a vacancy for a research student. The appointment had proved unpopular since it involved almost no clinical responsibility at all. Chatwyn took the post happily and spent the next eighteen months filing reports for the Assistant Professor who was preparing a monograph on the subject of placebo toxicity.

Then the Professor of Pharmacology obtained for him a grant from the Medical Research Council. The grant, for three years in the first instance, was to pay for research in the subject of paediatric cardio-pharmacology.

By the age of 40 Chatwyn was comfortably established as a research worker in a pleasant backwater of medical science.

* * *

Dr Singh was Dr Chatwyn's opposite in many respects. When he entered medical school his father had been a general practitioner for twenty-five years. Like all doctors' children entering medical school the young Singh had several immediate advantages; he knew what to expect and he had some slight tradition behind him to give him confidence. He was tall, blessed with a thick mop of black hair, and gregarious.

Singh was determined not to follow directly in his father's footsteps. He had, during his 'teens, seen his father's income and authority fall and his responsibilities rise. At the age of seventeen, he had to be moved from the public school where he had spent most of his school life, to a comprehensive school near to home. His father had been reluctant to allow him to attend medical school at all, but in the face of his son's determination, had made him promise to specialise.

Singh specialised in cardiac pharmacology, reasoning that, since cardiac diseases killed a high proportion of all men and women in the western world, there would for some years be a demand for specialists able to make some sense of the claims and counter-claims put forward by the numerous companies pitching for a share of the relevant drug market. At the age of 34 he had already been appointed a consultant in clinical pharmacology to a large general hospital; and had, in addition, a post as lecturer at the university where Dr Chatwyn worked. Unlike Dr Chatwyn, however, he found that his lectures were well attended.

In addition to these two jobs, Dr Singh acted as a consultant for numerous pharmaceutical companies, providing them with clinical research facilities and advice, and receiving in return considerable fees and opportunities to travel around the world. On each journey he usually managed to acquire an additional small commission to advise or provide information on some aspect of cardiac pharmacology.

At first sight these two doctors would seem to have little, apart from their professional interests, in common. They might seem improbable partners; Dr Chatwyn, shy and rather anxious to remain out of the limelight at all costs and Dr Singh, looking for material rewards for his professional skills.

In fact, when they met at a university faculty meeting that Dr Chatwyn had been quite unable to avoid, they quickly became friends. Dr Singh had almost unlimited access to commercial funds, and Dr Chatwyn, always looking for financial security to ensure that he would never be forced into looking for work as a practising doctor, had access to Medical Research Council facilities and could offer much in the way of accumulated knowledge. In addition, both bachelors enjoyed meetings abroad where they could live well and spend nothing.

0805 hrs. August 5th, Berkshire, England

'The subject spent the night in the Grand Hotel in Paris,' said the man. This one was very formal and he always referred to James as the subject. Cynthia didn't like his attitude at all. He somehow managed to make the whole wretched business seem even more distasteful than it was.

'He and his companion shared a room. Our representative

has photographs of the hotel register and signed statements from two members of the hotel staff.' The man paused for a moment. 'I'm afraid we had to make small payments to them,' he apologised. 'They were rather worried about the attitude of the management.'

'I see,' said Cynthia coolly. Now that she knew what was going on she felt far more capable of coping with it. She felt as though it was someone else's relationship she was studying; as thought it was someone else's marriage that she was watching split wide open.

'We'll continue to observe the subject's activities,' said the man. 'I'll report in twenty-four hours' time.'

'I'm going to Paris,' said Cynthia suddenly. She surprised even herself.

'No. I definitely wouldn't recommend that, Mrs Gower,' said the detective. He sounded rather agitated.

'It's my husband and I'm going to Paris,' said Cynthia firmly. The man's approach made her far more intransigent than she would normally have been. He started to protest again but she put the telephone down and silenced him. When it rang again a few moments later, she simply took it off the hook and left it lying on the table. She could hear him talking furiously; a thin, squeaky voice from some other world.

0812 hrs. August 5th, Athens, Greece

When the telephone rang, Merlin was quick to answer it. Merlin was a practical man and he knew when he had met his match. That man Bruckner wasn't the sort of fellow to play around with, he'd seen that.

'Mr Robert Merlin?' asked a polite male voice in perfect English.

'Speaking.'

'This is Paris calling,' continued the voice. 'I have the Transport Minister for you.' There were several clicks and then there was silence for a moment.

'I think you were expecting my call, Mr Merlin?'

Merlin agreed that he was.

'You'll be receiving a letter signed by me,' the Minister said. He spoke very quickly; rather nervously, Merlin thought. He wondered what hold Bruckner had over the Minister of Transport. He never doubted for one moment that there was something. 'I'd like you to act on it at the board meeting of the Channel Tunnel Company.'

'There will be no problems,' promised Merlin.

'I hope not,' said the Minister. There was a click and the line went dead. Merlin stared at the telephone receiver in his hand for several moments before carefully replacing it. If there had been any doubts in his mind about obeying Bruckner implicitly, there were none now. Merlin finished packing his case ready to fly to Paris.

0819 hrs. August 5th, Fontainebleau, France

The manager of the Palace Hotel in Fontainebleau prided himself on the food served to his guests. For five years the hotel had been the only one in the area to have a restaurant with the coveted three stars besides its name in the Michelin guide. Complaints were so rare and unusual that the hotel had no set procedure for dealing with them. No one could remember the last time anyone had the temerity to voice publicly any discontent about the hotel's culinary provisions. Tambroni, however, had no respect for the hotel, its reputation or its volatile and gifted chef.

'I ordered two boiled eggs and I told that man I wanted them boiled for three and a half minutes,' Tambroni shouted, pointing in the direction of an unfortunate red-faced waiter who had for ten minutes been at the receiving end of one of Tambroni's outbursts.

'On behalf of the management I apologise if you feel that you have not been properly suited,' said Guy Groult, the hotel manager. 'If you will allow me I will see that you are provided with eggs prepared precisely to your requirements.'

'The eggs were c... c... cooked to your sp... sp... specifications, sir,' stuttered the unhappy waiter.

'Don't lie to me!' screamed Tambroni. 'These eggs are hard and cold!'

'You were away from the table when I brought them into the dining room,' protested the waiter, losing his stutter in his indignation.

'Don't answer me back,' snapped Tambroni. He turned to the hotel manager, hovering unhappily nearby. 'Is this how you allow your staff to speak to your guests?' he demanded.

'I'm sure that M. Villiers was merely trying to ease the situation,' said the manager. He waved a hand to the waiter, dismissing him from the confrontation.

'You'll hear more about this,' Tambroni muttered. He stood up and pushed aside the eggs that had been the cause of so much trouble. Then he marched briskly out of the dining room. When he'd gone, Groult shrugged his shoulders and returned to his office. He passed the waiter who had been the butt of Tambroni's anger and smiled at him and raised an eyebrow.

Tambroni's tantrums were well known throughout the world. At one time, two or three years previously, he had hardly ever been out of the newspapers and magazines. He was a successful, professional squash player and had made a name for himself as a mean player and a poor loser in cities from Tokyo to Toronto.

Back in 1986, an attack of hepatitis had kept Tambroni out of major squash tournaments for four months. He hadn't started playing again until April 1987, when he'd entered for the Italian Open Championships in Turin. He'd been knocked out in the first round by an unknown amateur from Australia and he'd responded by smashing his racket against his opponent's shoulder. Even Tambroni's home crowd hadn't taken kindly to that. They'd even booed him off the court and two weeks later he'd been fined 1,000,000 lire by the sport's governing body. They'd also suspended him from international competitions.

After that Tambroni had returned to the club circuit. For ten months of the year he toured Europe, playing in private clubs and sometimes on public courts against local amateur sportsmen. They paid him a match fee and there were usually side bets which added to his income.

The Palace Hotel had a sports complex which included a nine-hole golf course, a heated swimming pool and a nest of six squash courts. One of the squash courts had a spectators' gallery capable of seating five hundred and it was there that Tambroni had been playing for the previous four days.

Now everyone was glad he was leaving for Paris. He was due to travel to England to play in a club in Wakefield for ten days.

Not, of course, that anyone at the Palace was unprofessional enough to allow Tambroni to realise that they were pleased to see him go. When he returned downstairs with his bags and ordered the hall porter to find him a taxi, he was greeted with deference and polite respect.

Not until an hour an a half later, when he had alighted from the train at the Gare de Lyon in Paris and climbed into a taxi to take him and his luggage to the Gare du Nord, did anyone say anything derogatory about their guest.

'I'd like to get his balls on the end of a squash racket,' said the hall porter to one of the assistant chefs in the staff dining room.

1030 hrs. August 5th, Paris

The offices of the Compagnie de Chemin de Fer Sous-marin Entre La France et L'Angleterre, known less formally and more affectionately as the Channel Tunnel Company, were situated in the place Vendôme, almost directly opposite the Ritz Hotel. On the ground floor, a decorative receptionist sat at a huge mahogany desk and gazed dispassionately at visitors who peered through the huge plate glass doors which fronted the reception area.

Behind the receptionist's desk were the publicity and press offices. There was in addition a small office occupied by a computer terminal which was directly linked to the main offices at Sangatte, and which provided up-to-date information about bookings and schedules.

The company had been launched jointly by the British and French Governments, and the Board, as well as commercial directors, included two spokesmen for each Government.

The British Government's two representatives were Lord Jack Kendall and Mr Robert Merlin. Although he had been on the board for two years, Kendall had yet to attend a meeting. He was primarily concerned with ensuring that the small but reassuringly regular fee, which his position on the board entitled him to collect, continued to appear in his bank account. With only a small pension from his union fund and a modest life insurance policy, Kendall's interest in the Channel Tunnel Company were personal.

Merlin, like Kendall, had received his place on the board as a token of thanks for services rendered in the past to his country's political life. That, at least, was the official line. Less generous commentators had suggested that Merlin had been appointed to the Tunnel's board because of the embarrassment he had caused his own party. As shadow Home Secretary and then a serving Chancellor of the Exchequer, Merlin had only just missed the highest office. His reputation with the party had always been that of an honest, zealous and loyal worker. Unfortunately, that reputation had been damaged by a series of revelations in an American news magazine. Merlin, it appeared, had for some time had an active account with a Swiss bank and he had, over a twelve-year period, speculated heavily on the European money market, using a broker in Switzerland, a false name and his numbered account.

The board of the Channel Tunnel Company also included three commercial representatives. Madame Janine Boysee, the only woman on the board, was the Marketing Director, responsible for promoting the tunnel's activities and ensuring that it acquired an increasing share of the cross-channel traffic. Sir Frederick Astor-Francis, secretary of the board, was the managing director of a small London bank which specialised in raising funds for international ventures. Besides the bank and the Channel Tunnel Company, Sir Frederick was a director of thirty-four other British and French companies. The other director with a special interest in finance was Herr Klaus Morgensdorf, whose career in European banking circles had become almost legendary. It was Morgensdorf who had helped arrange the loan from the European Credit Bank which had saved the British shipbuilding industry in 1981.

* * *

The first floor of the Channel Tunnel Company was occupied almost solely by the board room, an ornately furnished and decorated chamber.

The second and third floors contained the offices of the general manager and his staff. Originally it had been suggested that the general manager should be a full member of the board. The commercial directors had recommended this to the full board. They had, however, been overruled by the four political representatives, who, realising that as things were they had voting control, were unwilling to see that control threatened. The four political representatives were fully supported by their respective Governments, who realised that any general manager would undoubtedly be either French or British, and that consequently the delicate balance of French and British board members would be thrown out of alignment.

Thus, although the woman responsible for marketing the tunnel's services was a member of the board of directors (and had been a member since the tunnel had been first discussed as a realistic proposition), the general manager (who had only been appointed three months before the tunnel's completion) was not a member of the board and was not invited to attend meetings or to see copies of the minutes. It was a bizarre situation all too common in organisations run by two or more Governments.

The man with this position of responsibility with only limited authority, Philippe Garin, was in his early forties and had worked both for SNCF, the French national railways organisation, and for an international oil company. He had accepted the post as general manager of the Compagnie de Chemin de Fer Sous-marin Entre La France et L'Angleterre as a challenge. The very title of the company suggested a bureaucratic and administration-heavy organisation, and Garin's reputation had been built on his ability to create some sort of commercial order out of deliberately-arranged administrative chaos.

* * *

The board meeting was almost over.

'Well, gentlemen, is there any other business?' asked the chairman, Claude Noiret. He peered over his half-moon spectacles at each of the other board members. Since there weren't many members present it wasn't a habit that took up a great deal of time. Robert Merlin was the last of the three to receive Noiret's gaze, and he had already begun to gather up his papers and slide them to the narrow gold-clasped attaché case in front of him. Suddenly he stopped as though remembering something.

'I'm most dreadfully sorry,' he said. 'There is something. I almost forgot.' He took some papers out of his case and spread them out in front of him. 'A purely technical thing really, but one worth the board's attention and well worth getting out of the way today, in my opinion. I apologise for forgetting about it.'

The others, anxious to leave, said nothing but waited.

'Here it is,' said Merlin, picking up a sheaf of papers fixed together with a silver-coloured clip at the top left hand corner. 'Our transport schedule.'

'Surely we can't change that without a full meeting and until we've had prior consultation with the general manager and his staff?' asked Madame Boysee.

'Oh, I don't think we need worry too much about M. Garin as far as this is concerned,' smiled Merlin. 'It's more or less a technicality. Something that doesn't really have any practical significance.'

'I don't think we can change our schedule anyway without permission from the Ministry,' Noiret pointed out quietly.

'No problem at all,' insisted Merlin. He took a letter from his case and handed it across to the chairman. 'I had this yesterday. Full authorisation from the Minister himself for the changes proposed in the draft schedule.' He looked across at Noiret and smiled broadly.

'The authorisation is certainly adequate,' conceded Noiret. 'But what are the changes?'

'There's only one,' Merlin pointed out. 'It's on page 36 of the schedule and I've had photocopies – in English and French – made of the relevant page. He looked around and nodded at each of the others as he handed them photocopies of the pages to which he had referred. 'You will see,' he went on, 'that the amendment simply refers to pharmaceutical compounds. There were some restrictive clauses in the original schedule which should never had been passed in the first place. This is really just getting things in order.'

'I'm still not sure what it is we're talking about,' said Sir Frederick Astor-Francis, studying the schedule.

'The original schedule restricted the transport of certain chemicals,' explained Merlin. 'And of course there were very good reasons for the restrictive clauses. I'm not arguing with those at all. We don't want our trains carrying explosives in the tunnel, do we?'

No one said anything.

'The problem is simply that, along with the more dangerous chemicals, we've restricted the types of pharmaceuticals we can transport; medically required drugs and so on.'

'The Minister has agreed to the change,' said Noiret, putting down the letter that Merlin had handed to him. Merlin handed the letter across the table to Sir Frederick who read it through quickly before handing it back.

'You mean we're not allowing drug companies to transport their medicinal compounds?' asked Morgensdorf, speaking for the first time.

'That's right,' nodded Merlin. 'It's pretty obvious that a load of heart pills isn't going to be dangerous, but we've legislated against them in our original schedule.' He shrugged. 'It's just a technical error.'

'I think we ought to let M. Garin have a look at this first,' suggested Madame Boysee.

'Oh, I really don't think we need to do that,' said Noiret. 'It has been passed by the Minister.'

'And the suggested change did come from him,' said Merlin. 'The revised schedule came through his office.'

'Really?' said Noiret, raising an eyebrow and then lowering it again quickly. Alone of those present, he wondered why the recommendation had been made to Merlin and not to him. Noiret didn't like things he didn't understand. But whatever was going on he had no intention of getting in the way at this stage. 'Well, let's take a vote on it now, shall we?'

'I propose that we accept the new schedule,' suggested Morgensdorf.

'I'll second that,' said Merlin.

'Right,' said Noiret. 'That's settled then.' He didn't wait for the other two to offer opinions. Nor did he give an opinion himself. 'Shall we declare the meeting closed?'

He began to shuffle his papers together, and wondered whom to ring at the Transport Ministry.

1050 hrs. August 5th, Zürich, Switzerland

From his office at the southern corner of the 16th floor of the ACR Drogue et Cie building at Zürich, Albert Huber stared down at the slow-moving traffic in the streets below. Red and white Swiss national flags hung out of almost every window in sight as a lasting memory of the country's national Confederation Day, celebrated four days previously. The flags would be brought indoors soon, since the Swiss disliked any excessive show of emotion or patriotism. Besides, if the flags were left out too long, they would become tattered and dirty and need replacing for next year's celebrations.

'I've brought your coffee, Herr Huber,' whispered Miss Bird, the company chairman's confidential secretary. She carefully put down a rosewood tray on a glass-topped onyx table, adjusted the three cups and saucers on the tray and plugged the percolator into a socket fitted into the top of the table.

'Thank you,' said the chairman without turning round. His two guests, Dr Jackson, the company's medical director, and Willy Meier, the company's marketing director, both smiled at Miss Bird. Jackson murmured thanks.

'It looks as if we'll be operational in the United Kingdom within a week,' said Meier, when the secretary had left.

'How's the promotion gone over there?' asked Huber. He still didn't turn around. He seemed to be hypnotised by the activities of a motorist looking for a parking pace in the Bahnhofstrasse. The motorist might as well have been looking for gold on the pavements of London.

'They're just waiting for the stuff,' said Jackson cheerfully.

He was permanently optimistic and the success of the early trials of Angipax had left him without a single qualm or reservation.

'How long will it take to set up the machinery?' Herr Huber asked.

'I'll have the machinery moved from Finchley tomorrow,' said Jackson. 'We can be operational forty-eight hours after we move into the factory.'

'What about the raw materials?' asked Bruckner. 'We still haven't got the chemicals over there.'

'They're ready to move,' said Jackson. 'I've just had confirmation.'

'Wasn't there some problem with the channel tunnel people?'

'Sorted,' said Jackson.

'We're promising to have the finished product ready on the pharmacists' shelves by the 25th,' said Meier.

'We'll make that easily,' nodded Jackson. 'There's no problem with that.'

'We could move some supplies over just in case,' said Meier. 'Just a few thousand cartons.'

'No.' said Herr Huber, shaking his head.

The others looked at him.

'We're not moving any finished tablets into the country,' said the chairman. 'There's too much risk of the British Government interfering with our pricing arrangements,' he explained. 'If we move raw supplies over there then we have no problems. If we sell the basic chemicals in a pure form to a solely British subsidiary, we can get grants from the British Government and claim tax relief on our entire investment. We can also sell the chemicals to our British subsidiary at a considerable profit, bringing the bulk of the money we make in the UK back to Switzerland and France where the Governments are rather less punitive in their taxes.' He smiled.

'And we can also get a Common Market grant because we're moving into a depressed area,' said Jackson, also with a smile. 'The whole thing is beautiful.'

'I'd better be moving,' said Meier standing up and looking at his watch. 'Will you excuse me, sir?' he said to Herr Huber.

'I've got to look at a film we've had made for free distribution to post-graduate centres in Britain.'

'Certainly, Willy,' said the chairman. 'Marvellous work you've been doing.'

'I'd better get these chemicals on the road,' said Jackson.

The two men left.

Only then did the chairman turn away from the window. He pressed a button on the telephone on his desk. Moments later he was speaking to a banker and discussing the details of the advantages his company could obtain by selling the company's short-term loan bonds to an Italian bank owned entirely by a select group of the board of the main company.

1055 hrs. August 5th, rue Mont Thabor, Paris

'May I leave my suitcases there for a moment?' Cater asked the clerk at the small hotel where he'd been staying.

'Certainly,' nodded the clerk.

'I've just got a few bits of shopping to do,' explained Cater. He'd already paid the hotel bill through the travel agency who'd made all the arrangements on his behalf.

He'd bought and posted cards on his first day in Paris. Cards to each of the children, to Julie and to the secretary in the office. But he'd forgotten to buy them any presents. It wasn't so much that he'd forgotten – more that he'd never managed to make his mind up what to buy. He walked from the rue Mont Thabor along the rue de Castiglione and into the rue de Rivoli. It was fairly early in the morning for Paris and the shops were still more or less deserted. He stopped at half-a-dozen souvenir shops, and looked at the toys and gifts for sale. Eventually he called in at a souvenir and book shop and bought English story books at vastly inflated prices and four models of the Eiffel Tower in a snowstorm. He felt embarrassed as he paid for them but at least he'd got something.

Then he walked back along the rue de Rivoli. He still had to get something for Julie. He stopped outside a shop selling exotic female underwear, and stared at the astonishing variety of silky garments they had on sale. Suddenly, on impulse, he walked in. He stood for a moment just inside the shop, uncertain about what he intended to buy. He'd been attracted by a set of matching red bra and panties worn by a transparent plastic model in the window. But when the assistant, a middle-aged woman with purple hair, came to serve him he lost his nerve.

'Do you sell scarves?' he asked.

The woman produced a tray of hideously decorated scarves, all printed with pictures of animals or birds. He bought the one that he thought Julie would like most, and then called in at another shop a little further on and bought a bottle of perfume.

Back at the hotel the clerk was still studying the newspaper. Cater said nothing but picked up his two suitcases, one of which was full of copies of books. He then walked along to the Tuileries Métro station and took the Metro to the Gare du Nord. He had to change at the Concorde station and, while dragging the two suitcases from platform to platform along, seemingly, unending corridors, he cursed himself for not taking a taxi. At the Gare du Nord he bought a couple of paperbacks and some magazines, then joined the train leaving for the tunnel terminal.

1115 hrs. August 5th, Paris

Noiret was confused. He had telephoned the Transport Ministry and discovered that the Minister had written to Merlin entirely on his own initiative. No one else in the department seemed to know anything about it.

Noiret, who knew when to make a noise and when to keep quiet, decided to keep quiet. There are times when discretion is the basis for survival.

1130 hrs. August 5th, place de l'Opéra, Paris

On the pavement in front of the Paris Opera House a hundred hands fumbled with umbrella catches.

James Gower and Hélène Albric had no umbrella and did not even have raincoats with them. Hélène pulled her woollen shawl tightly round her slim bare shoulders and shivered twice, quickly in succession. Holding hands, they picked their way in between the other patrons. They were staying at the Grand Hotel, only a few metres away, and they hurried into the side entrance.

'Coffee?' asked James, helping Hélène to unwrap her shawl. It was pleasantly warm in the foyer.

'I'd like a brandy,' whispered Hélène, slipping her hand between James' arm and his body. They walked together through the hotel's glass-fronted restaurant. Several people looked in Hélène's direction. She had delicate, doll-like features which always brought stares of admiration. James Gower, clearly in his fifties, attracted only knowing smiles.

A white coated waiter hurried to them as they sat down. James ordered two glasses of Camus Napoléon and black coffee for them both. The rain had begun to fall a little harder and, outside, the pedestrians were hurrying to complete their journeys before they became soaked. Unusually, the fashionable shops in the Avenue de l'Opéra were attracting no window shoppers.

Inside, it was warm and comfortable and made even more so by the knowledge that outside it was cold and wet. As James and Hélène watched a middle-aged man struggling with an umbrella which had blown inside out by a sudden gust of wind, the waiter arrived with their brandy and coffee. He placed the glasses and cups on the table and quietly slipped the bill into James' saucer.

Hélène Albric had acquired a good knowledge of the world's great art while travelling through the European capitals with her father, who had been a career diplomat. Her mother had gone off with an Austrian businessman when Hélène had been nine, and had maintained a steady disinterest in her daughter's welfare thereafter. As an only child with a single parent, Hélène's education in matters both academic and domestic had been unusual, to say the least. She had been fortunate, however, in that her father had a passionate interest in art and artists.

He had died in a motor car accident when she was twenty, leaving her very well off in monetary terms but quite deprived in terms of love and affection. She had never spent much time with any other relatives and such attachments as she had made had been brief and emotionally unimportant.

She'd gone to live in London, taking a small flat in South Kensington, and had found a job working in James Gower's gallery in Regent Street. She'd been working there for nearly a month before she even met Gower. When she did, she found herself attracted to him and she knew that he found her attractive. He invited her out to dinner on the first evening that they met and afterwards they spent the night at a small flat he had in Mayfair mews.

* * *

James Gower had arrived in London at the age of twenty-two with a suitcase of clothes, and a diploma in design in his pocket. He'd taken a job as a window dresser with a large London store and had spent his first month's wages on buying himself a Savile Row suit, a pair of Savile Row shoes and an expensive silk tie and shirt from the Burlington Arcade. Then he'd deliberately and systematically proceeded to make the acquaintance of every half-pretty, wealthy young woman in London.

It hadn't been too difficult. There were always plenty of horsy young women and their mothers taking tea in Fortnum and Mason's in the afternoon, and Gower would slip out of the store for an hour and take tea alongside them. After a few weeks he was on nodding terms with several. At the end of a month he chose one, introduced himself, apologised for his impertinence and boldness, and arranged a dinner date at one of London's most exclusive restaurants. The bill had exceeded his income for the week but it had been worth it. Six weeks later, James Gower and Cynthia Mitchell had been married in a small country church in Berkshire. The wedding was reported in *The Tatler* and *Country Life*, and it was noted that the couple were spending their honeymoon in Tahiti.

When they arrived back in London, Cynthia's father was persuaded to part with enough money to enable Gower to open a small art gallery in a side street near Grosvenor Square. From then on, Gower's raw ability to make money had taken over. Within a decade he had a business grossing over a million pounds a year. Unfortunately, he still had Cynthia, and since Cynthia's father was no fool, he had no chance of ever getting rid of her. Mrs Gower was the holder of 50% of the shares in the company James Gower had formed when buying his first shop. Every penny he had made was tied up in that small company and a break with his wife would have proved disastrous.

So, Gower remained a more or less faithful husband, staying in London to attend to business just two or three days a week, and speeding back to the country to spend the evening with his wife in their spacious country home on the other days.

The trip to Paris had been Hélène's idea. She insisted on it, in fact. James had finally agreed when his wife had announced that she had been invited to spend three days at a health farm in Dorset with her cousin.

'Well, I have been wanting to go over to Paris and look at a few pieces by a couple of new artists,' James had murmured.

'Do you mind, dear?' asked Cynthia. 'I feel awful just going off and leaving you.'

'You won't be leaving me,' insisted James. 'I'll go and stay at a hotel in Paris.'

Cynthia, apparently innocent and unsuspecting, gave her husband a peck on the cheek and told him how lucky she was to have such an understanding husband. James wandered down to the village post-box, with his Great Danes as an excuse, and telephoned Hélène. She'd been deliriously happy when he'd told her the good news.

1143 hrs. August 5th, Hotel Continental, Paris

The journal that Dr Singh held was printed on expensive glossy paper and filled with highly coloured graphs. The title, *The International Journal of Cardiac Pharmacology* was printed discreetly in the top centre of the front page, and beneath it, as is customary with so many technical journals, there was a list of the major articles appearing in the journal. Dr Singh's right forefinger prodded repeatedly at the title of an article which he himself had written, and which described in glowing scientific detail the many advantages of the new drug 'Angipax'.

'They liked it, then?' asked Dr Singh, who had just finished describing to the ACR Drogues' senior Northern European representative just how difficult it was to get an article published in such a well-esteemed specialist journal.

'Very pleased with it,' nodded Ernest Taylor, the drug company representative who was well accustomed to dealing with egotistical medical specialists, and who considered himself to be something of an expert at commercial obsequiousness. Like any competent car salesman, he always managed to find a consuming interest which he could share with his customers, but, unlike an ordinary salesman, he had the extra imagination to ensure that he never knew quite so much about their mutual interest as his customer. This talent enabled him to imbue his customers both with sympathy and a real feeling of superiority.

Dr Singh all but purred with satisfaction.

'I hope your people haven't forgotten that little arrangement we have,' he said, carefully putting the copy of the *International Journal of Cardiac Pharmacology* back into his Dunhill document case, itself a gift six months previously from Taylor himself.

'Of course not,' said Taylor quickly. 'Our medical director , however, did wonder if you felt it entirely sensible, considering all the circumstances.'

'What do you mean?' frowned Singh, edging forward and breathing clouds of stale brandy into the representative's face. Taylor didn't flinch. 'We had an arrangement, didn't we?'

'Of course we did,' agreed Taylor. 'And no one is trying to break the arrangement. We just wanted to be absolutely certain that you felt that nothing had changed.'

'Why should anything have changed?'

'I don't know,' said Taylor. 'You're the expert, doctor,' he added quickly with a sycophantic smile. Personally, Taylor had felt the arrangement to be a bad one when the company's medical director had made it with Singh. But it wasn't his job to quarrel with the medical director; especially when Dr Singh had just produced an article in a major specialist journal which would give them notable references to quote on world-wide advertising literature.

So the agreement had been made and, although it had never been put on to paper, for reasons that were only too obvious to everyone concerned, ACR Drogues et Cie were morally committed to providing Dr Singh with one vial of smallpox virus. Presuming, that is, that one can have a moral commitment to an illegal act.

'We're doing research into the efficacy of a new anti-viral drug we've developed,' Singh had said. 'And since the disaster in Birmingham ten years ago, the World Health Organisation hasn't allowed researchers access to the smallpox virus. Our virus man says there just isn't anything more suitable for the research we're doing. I don't suppose you have a supply do you?'

Taylor had referred the specialist to his own medical director, Dr Jackson, and the three of them had met ten months previously in a hotel in Geneva. There, Dr Jackson had confirmed that the company did indeed have its own private stock of smallpox virus, but had pointed out that holding the stock, let alone allowing it to be used, was prohibited by the 1982 Geneva Research Convention.

Singh in turn had pointed out that he had recently been appointed an international editor of two leading medical journals, and that neither he nor his colleagues intended to do anything dishonourable with the virus. 'We only want it for valuable medical research,' he said, 'This is life-saving stuff we're doing. If we can develop this anti-viral agent, it could be the biggest breakthrough since penicillin. Our specialist feels that another two years' work could see him well on the way.'

Dr Jackson had agreed that an effective anti-viral with wide-ranging uses would be both clinically and commercially valuable. In return for a signed, witnessed contract giving ACR Drogues the legal right to exploit commercially any product developed within Singh's laboratory on payment of a royalty, Dr Jackson had personally authorised the withdrawal of a vial of smallpox virus from the ACR laboratory in Basle.

And clearly, Singh had not forgotten the arrangement, as Taylor had rather hopelessly prayed that he might.

In his three-room suite at the Continental, Taylor handed over a small steel case to Singh. It looked about the same size as an ordinary pocket cigarette lighter.

'Look after it!' said Taylor as he handed the case over. Singh looked at him in surprise. He wasn't used to this side of Taylor. 'There hasn't been a case of smallpox in the world for a decade now, said Taylor. If you let this stuff out, you'd do more damage than Attila the Hun.'

Singh began to mutter something but thought better of it. He took the case from Taylor and stuffed it into his pocket. He didn't intend to start taking advice from drug company representatives, but neither did he want to upset Taylor. He enjoyed the good life that ACR helped him live.

1200 noon August 5th, Sangatte, France

The Blacks arrived at Sangatte at noon.

'You're lucky,' said the clerk, 'We can get your car and caravan on the six o'clock freight train.' He took the Blacks' tickets and told Mr Black to drive to Bay 3. 'You'll have to leave your vehicle there,' he said. 'And then travel in the passenger train.'

'Stop for a minute, dear,' said Mrs Black as they approached the signs announcing the various loading bays.

'Stop?'

'I want to just check the things in the caravan,' explained Mrs Black. 'It won't take me a minute.' Mr Black pulled the car into the side of the road.

Inside the caravan Mrs Black scurried around making sure that all lockable cupboards were firmly locked and that the bed linen was neatly folded in the storage bins underneath the bunks. The caravan smelt of dampness as a result of the wet clothes which were scattered about the floor and across the towel-protected upholstery. The clothes she'd been trying to dry were still as wet as they had been to begin with. Sighing and shaking her head unhappily, Mrs Black opened one of the drawers in the cupboard underneath the stove and found a box of matches. Lighting a match she held the flame above the gas ring at the front of the stove. The bright blue flame appeared on the stove just as the match was about to go out. Putting the matches back into the drawer, Mrs Black moved several items of clothing nearer to the stove. She put a sweater of her husband's on top of the grill and draped one of her own pairs of slacks over the spare gas cylinder which was standing in the middle of the caravan's narrow passageway. Having done that she went around the caravan drawing all the curtains.

'There,' she said finally to herself. 'They should be nice and dry by the time we get to England and no one will be any the wiser.' Then she climbed out of the caravan, locked the door and went back to the car.

At Bay 3 the Blacks left their car in the care of a balding middle-aged Frenchman whose wife had given him sardine paste sandwiches for the third time in a week and who was not in a good mood. He drove the Black's car on to the train with less care than he would have usually taken, and Mr Black's sweater moved forwards slightly on the grill. The car and caravan were last on to the part of the train occupied by passenger cars. To complete the train, sixteen freight wagons were attached to it.

1400 hrs. August 5th, Gare due Nord, Paris

Mrs Gower had watched her husband and Hélène Albric board the train in Paris from the station buffet. She'd spotted her husband's expensive overcoat almost as soon as the two travellers had entered the station. When they'd boarded she followed, sitting in a compartment two carriages ahead of them.

She didn't know why she was there or what she planned to do. She simply knew that she had to see them for herself. Somehow it seemed like watching someone else's husband; like seeing someone else's marriage collapsing. She didn't feel as sad or as unhappy as she'd thought she would. There wasn't even any humiliation or sense of defeat.

If any emotion was dominant it was pity. Pity for her husband not herself. She felt sorrow for him, having to search for happiness and fulfilment with a woman young enough to be his daughter. But even that emotion seemed to be felt through a mist. It was all strangely unreal.

1625 hrs. August 5th, Sangatte, France

The Sangatte Tunnel Terminal had been designed to take full

advantage of all available technological aids. Passengers arriving by road or rail from seventeen different directions were brought speedily and easily into the heart of the terminal, where they could board the Tunnel train. There were stations connecting with Paris, Brussels and Luxembourg. Freight was brought into the terminal either by road or rail. Only freight travelling in containers suitable for both road and rail transportation was accepted.

Unfortunately, despite (or perhaps because of) the variety of available technical aids, the tunnel was subject to the usual mechanical problems. This time it was the tunnel's emergency lighting system, in which the central control computer had diagnosed a fault. A team of engineers were working in the tunnel and trains were temporarily suspended.

The express from Paris had been due in Sangatte at five minutes to four. The passengers included the elderly English pilgrim, Miss Millington; Peter Cater, the publisher; the two British doctors, Dr Chatwyn and Dr Singh who had been attending the Angipax conference in Paris; the Italian squash player Tambroni; the computer manager Alan Cannon and the art gallery owner, James Gower, and his mistress, Hélène Albric. Their train arrived on the outskirts of the Sangatte terminal on time but, owing to the fact that the trains which had arrived at five minutes to three and twenty five minutes past three were still in the station disgorging their passengers, the station was unable to accommodate them. The 350 passengers had to sit and wait, with varying degrees of patience.

1740 hrs. August 5th, Tunnel maintenance

The maintenance crew foreman swore angrily and threw his automatic screwdriver into the metal box he used to carry his tools. For the fifth time in an hour, a screw had snapped. When they'd started work an hour earlier it had seemed a simple problem. The alternative lighting circuit seemed to have developed a short, but they still had not discovered the source of the fault; all they had managed to do was to take three roofing panels down, and at the rate they were going they'd still be working in another three hours. The Tunnel's management would never accept that. The foreman, together with his colleagues, had been subjected to a long harangue from Raspail immediately after lunch. The engineer had made it clear that the Tunnel had to be kept closed for as little time as possible.

'We're never going to finish this tonight,' called the older of the two other crew members, a middle-aged Breton.

'The football starts in an hour and a half,' moaned his younger colleague, a youth called Tony who wore small gold earrings and played for the Sangatte football team. The match he referred to, however, was due to be played on television rather than the local pitch.

'Come on then,' said the foreman, easily persuaded. He picked up his tool box and made his way towards the connecting passage which would take them back to the pilot tunnel. In there waited their small working engine. The other two men walked quickly after him, pausing only to snatch up their own tool and luncheon bags.

'What about the ceiling panels?' asked the Breton. 'We're supposed to put them back on, aren't we?'

'It's just taken all day to get them off,' pointed out the youth.

The foreman stopped, turned round and stared balefully at the three ceiling panels which were stacked neatly on the narrow catwalk.

'No one's going to see them,' the youth pointed out. 'And if we put them back it'll probably take us another five hours.'

'Leave them off,' said the Breton, half regretting his first comment. 'You're right. No one's going to notice anyway.' They all knew that since all the trains which travelled in the tunnel were windowless, there was little chance of anyone noticing that the panels had been left out of position.

'At least we'll be able to get on with it straight away tomorrow,' rationalised the foreman. 'It'll save time and that should please Raspail.' He walked off again and the other two men followed him gratefully.

1753 hrs. August 5th, Sangatte, France

At a few minutes before six on the evening of the 5th August, the two containers from the ACR factory at St Quentin en Yvelines were hitched onto the train at Sangatte. They were placed at the front of the freight wagons in view of the fact that the freight manager himself had taken an interest in them and had insisted that they be given priority. His interest meant that the ACR drugs were directly behind the Black's caravan.

1820 hrs. August 5th, Sangatte, France

The fault which had kept the passengers on the 14.00 express from Paris fuming in their compartments had caused a two-hour delay. Miss Millington, Alan Cannon, Dr Chatwyn and Dr Singh, Sr. Tambroni, James Gower and Hélène Albric all joined the 18.20 passenger train from Sangatte in France to Westernhanger in England. Those seven, together with Peter Cater, Susan Roberts, Gaston Raenackers and the four members of the Black family, made up the passengers in compartment 22 on the train which left just after the freight train.

Each passenger compartment was quite self-contained, with five rows of seats, each row containing five individual seats. To facilitate boarding, the entire sides of each compartment lifted up allowing passengers to board from either side of their own particular row. The fact that the sides of the compartments lifted in their entirety made central aisles quite unnecessary and obviated the need for connecting doors. During each journey the passengers inside every compartment were effectively imprisoned in a plastic cocoon.

The Black family took up four of the five front seats. The fifth seat on their row was unoccupied. Behind them sat two people: Dr Singh and Dr Chatwyn. The two doctors sat together in the two left-hand seats, leaving the three seats on their right unoccupied. In the middle row there were no empty seats. James Gower and Hélène Albric occupied the two seats on the left of Miss Millington, and Alan Cannon and Peter Cater occupied the two seats on her right. The fourth or penultimate row was occupied by Benito Tambroni, who sat alone in the centre seat and scowled at anyone who approached him. In the last row, occupying the seats on the left, sat Susan Roberts and Gaston Raenackers.

There were, then, fourteen people in the compartment and eleven empty seats.

* * *

For the first few miles from the terminal at Sangatte the train ran above ground; at the Tunnel portal the train disappeared from view for the first time. The tracks slowly descended so that at the coast the tunnel was about thirty metres below the sea bed. The freight train arrived at the tunnel portal at 6.20 pm, just as the passenger train was leaving the terminal. Three and a half minutes later, with the freight train nearing the French coast the passenger train passed into the underground tunnel. The driver of the passenger train, George Philpot, whose only task was to keep an eye on the computerised controls and, in case of any systems fault, release the dead man's handle which would automatically bring the train to a halt, saw that the driverless freight train was three and a half minutes ahead. At 6.30 pm both trains were thirty metres or more underneath the English Channel and heading for the English coast at speeds of approximately 100 kilometres per hour.

Inside the Black's caravan the wet clothes which Mrs Black had left drying over the stove were steaming as they dried. Mr Black's sweater which had been resting on top of the grill was very nearly dry. While the train had been standing in the terminal station it had still been quite securely draped over the grill. However, as the train accelerated towards the Tunnel portal, it began to slip. By the time the train had reached the coast the left-hand sleeve had fallen off the grill and was dangling about two inches above the naked flame of the stove.

The sweater fell on to the flame three miles out from the French coast. If it had fallen off the grill a little earlier it might have been wet enough to extinguish the small flame of the stove. As it was it caught fire almost instantaneously. As the flames wrapped around the sweater the whole bundle of woollen fire fell off the stove and on to the top of the spare gas cylinder which was standing in the caravan aisle. Since the gas cylinder was made of thick steel, that in itself might have not proved too bad, had not Mrs Black left a pair of her own slacks resting on top of it. The burning sweater knocked the slacks off the cylinder and fell with them on to the floor. The slacks, which were also nearly dry, caught fire within seconds and soon the carpet on which they had both landed was also ablaze. Three minutes later, the whole of the caravan interior was burning.

In the passenger train Mrs Black was handing a tin of boiled sweets around the compartment. Apart from the squash player in the fourth row and Miss Roberts and Gaston Raenackers on the fifth row, everyone in the compartment had accepted a sweet and Mrs Black was purring contentedly with a sense of public spirit.

The fire in the Blacks' caravan raged with astonishing speed and, within a few minutes, the caravan itself was completely destroyed. The destruction of the vehicle had been expedited by the fact that a few seconds after the blazing sweater hit the floor the gas cylinder supplying the stove exploded. The cylinder ignited quickly because the value which supplied the stove had, of course, been left open by Mrs Black.

The explosion involving the gas cylinder not only destroyed the caravan but also involved the Blacks' Peugeot car in the blaze. The car's petrol tank was about two metres away from the exploding gas cylinder and it quickly ignited. The car was blown half out of the restraining chains which were intended to keep it firmly in place during the journey, and the rear of the car was blown out through the opaque green plastic wall of the car container.

The overhead sprinklers came into operation as soon as the heat sensors in the tunnel ceiling registered the rise in temperature. Unfortunately the sprinklers had been designed to cope with a static fire, and the two-second delay before they came into operation meant that the freight train was well out of range by the time each set of sprinklers came into action.

All might still have been well if there had not been a second potential bomb in the Blacks' caravan. The second, spare cylinder of gas had not exploded at first but, as the heat inside the remains of the caravan continued to rise, the temperature of the gas increased and finally the cylinder did explode. If it hadn't done so then there might perhaps have been a chance that the disaster would have been limited to the freight train.

The explosion of the second gas cylinder had two effects. The fire, which had previously been confined to the freight trailer containing the Blacks' car and caravan, finally spread both forwards and backwards.

A piece of the exploding gas cylinder shot forwards through the plastic of the next freight container and into the last of the three cars it contained. Within seconds, that car was ablaze and shortly afterwards the two cars in front of them also exploded. The combined heat and force generated by three exploding petrol tanks proved too much for the plastic walls of the freight container and the cars in the next compartment exploded less than ten seconds later. Within less than a minute the whole of the freight train was ablaze.

It was the second of the Blacks' two gas cylinders which caused the major explosion. The cylinder had exploded downwards, fired by the release of gas through the weaker part, the uppermost valve. The cylinder had gone straight through the bogie and had crashed on to the rails. From there is had bounced backwards, meeting the next part of the train.

The bouncing cylinder had severed the coupling between the trailer which had contained the Blacks' caravan and the following trailer. The forward part of the train had continued on its way, accelerating slightly as it abandoned its rearmost portion. The latter part or the train had begun to slow down, moving only because of its own momentum.

Three of the freight trailers carried metal spare parts for motor cars; two held tyres, and another contained urgently-needed copies of European Economic Community publications. None of these commodities was highly inflammable, any more than were the two containers full of tea and the three cylinders full of farm produce. If the bouncing cylinder had ended its erratic journey in any of these containers there would have been no further explosion.

Unfortunately, the tyres, the motor car parts, the EEC

publications, the farm produce and the tea were not in the container next to the Blacks' car and caravan. The first of the freight containers was filled, not with inert fruit or documents, but with raw chemicals. The erythrytyl tetranitrate and the pentaerythritol tetranitrate were destined for a peaceful life as constituents of Angipax, Europe's newest and latest best-selling heart drug, but they were both highly explosive substances, closely allied in chemical form to the substance known to explosive experts as TNT.

The bouncing cylinder hit the freight compartment at a relative speed of over 250 kilometres per hour. It crashed into the freight container at the junction of its base and leading wall. The red hot cylinder acted like a detonator as it compressed the erythrytyl tetranitrate and the resulting explosion involved every gramme of the chemical.

Within the confined area of the underground railway tunnel the results of the explosion were devastating. The tunnel roof collapsed and the blast wave lifted both the departing front half of the freight train and the engine and the first nine compartments of the approaching passenger train a full metre off the railway tracks.

Inside the control room at Sangatte, where the duty controller was munching a cheese and tomato sandwich, the computer screens suddenly went blank. The controller was unperturbed.

'Systems fault.' he called out, automatically reaching forward to switch in an auxiliary system.

* * *

The tunnel was built like a huge tube, seven metres in diameter, and the trains ran on rails laid on a floor that measured five metres across. The roof of the tunnel was made of precast concrete pieces bolted together with mild steel plates fixed as an internal facing. The plates were galvanised on the inside and each weighed four tons. Apart from the driver's cab the passenger train consisted of 22 compartments, each containing a potential of 25 passengers. The passengers in each of the first 21 compartments died instantly as the train and the steel segments collided in mid air. Released by the collapse of the roof, limestone and clay burst into the tunnel instantaneously. The passenger compartments, made of aluminium and plastic for weight economy, provided no protection at all against the falling steel and rock. Three hundred and ninety three passengers, the total number of people travelling in the first 21 compartments, died.

The explosion ripped the electrical wiring and water sprinkler systems into a thousand pieces and the whole of the tunnel was suddenly pitch black. The whole disaster, from the moment Mr Black's sweater had first fallen from the grill in the caravan, had taken less than two minutes.

Between the tunnel which was now effectively destroyed, and the parallel tunnel used for the transport of people and goods from England to France, there were connecting passageways every three hundred metres. These narrow passageways were intended to provide maintenance crews and emergency squads with access from one tunnel to the other; they were fixed at right angles to the main tunnels and connected first with a pilot tunnel some three metres in diameter. The centre of the pilot tunnel was approximately fifteen metres away from the centre of each of the two main tunnels. Since the main tunnels were seven metres each in width and the pilot tunnel three metres in width at its widest point, this meant that the connecting passageways were about ten metres in length. Theoretically, these connecting passageways would, in the case of any accident or tunnel collapse, (both rendered unlikely by the enormous number of safety precautions built into the system) enable passengers and rescuers to move freely from tunnel to tunnel. They would also enable workmen to maintain a good supply of fresh air to all parts of the tunnel through an extensive system of ventilator shafts and ducts.

Unfortunately, the explosion had also destroyed many of the connecting tunnels. In addition, the roof of the France-bound tunnel was slightly cracked in several places and numerous falls of rocks and clay had already occurred.

Miraculously, almost unbelievably, the explosion had left one small pocket of life untouched.

In front of compartment 22 the roof of the tunnel had given way completely in several places. Huge steel plates were buckled and bent like pieces of tin foil. The tunnel was full of rocks. Behind compartment 22 the blast wave had opened several small gaps in the tunnel roof through which tons of soft clay had fallen. The channel bed is composed of many different types of rock and earth. Directly above the leading part of the train there was little but limestone; behind it the tunnel roof was supporting several million tons of clay. The first collapse allowed limestone rocks into the tunnel; the second breach, caused by the blast wave, brought in several hundred tons of clay, which, reinforced by the pressure of solid clay above it, spread slowly towards both coasts. By a remarkable fluke, compartment 22 was trapped between the fall of limestone and the fall of clay; as the clay crept forwards it compressed the air that had been caught in the tunnel so that outside compartment 22 the air pressure reached a level several times that inside the compartment.

The explosion had knocked compartment 22 off its rails and on to its side. It leant against the side of the tunnel with a small pocket of air trapped underneath it in a triangular space which was filling slowly with clay and small pieces of rock. Because the air was under tremendous pressure, however, the clay advanced only slowly, creeping along the tunnel floor quite imperceptibly.

Inside the compartment there was bedlam. The compartment itself, now in total darkness, was tilted to the right and the passengers who had been sitting in the left hand seats had been thrown onto their neighbours' laps.

The noise was deafening for a few moments and then in contrast there was a silence and the silence itself was unnatural. Louise Black sobbed hysterically and her mother muttered useless words of encouragement to her.

'Dear me,' said Miss Millington, rather loudly. 'I do apologise to whoever I'm sitting on.'

* * *

The duty controller decided that something other than a systems failure had caused his blank screens. He pressed the emergency button, and the train travelling to France from England stopped two miles out from the English coast.

1840 hrs. August 5th, Sangatte, France

At both Sangatte and Westernhanger there were three terminal managers, working on eight-hour shifts, responsible for the train leaving and arriving at their terminals. A resident engineer and safety officer, both having offices at Sangatte, were responsible for all the problems within their special areas of authority. The terminal managers were simply expected to ensure that the trains arrived and left on time and that passengers boarding and leaving main-line trains were taken through the tunnel as quickly and as efficiently as possible. They were, of course, also responsible for looking after freight transportation.

When the duty controller at Sangatte had pressed the emergency button, the duty manager, sitting in his office sorting and signing requisition orders and supply control order forms, was instantly informed of the potential emergency by the sound of a buzzer on his intercom. A small red light on his desk provided visual reinforcement of the audible signal. The duty manager, Charles Martini, picked up the telephone on his desk and was immediately put through to the control room.

'I think we have some sort of failure, sir,' reported the duty controller. 'The screens on the outgoing line have gone blank.'

'What about the emergency system?'

'Nothing,' said the controller. 'We have total failure.'

'I'll be right there,' promised the duty manager. He put down his telephone, left his office and walked along to the control room less than fifty metres away. There he discovered that only the television cameras covering the lines in the first half-kilometre of the outward tunnel were operational, that the remainder of the electrical systems supplying the outward-bound tunnel and the pilot tunnel were completely dead, and that the main electrical supply to the inward tunnel was only functioning haphazardly. The main systems in the inward tunnel were also quite dead. It was clear that the fault was a major one and the duty manager decided to report immediately to the headquarters in the place Vendôme. Nine minutes after the explosion on the train out of Sangatte, a telex message was received in the Paris offices of the Channel Tunnel Company. In Paris, as well as

Sangatte and Westernhanger, the computer terminals and telex machine were staffed for twenty-four hours a day.

Acting in accordance with the standing instructions the telex operator immediately rang Garin's private telephone number, and twenty-four minutes after the undersea explosion, the Channel Tunnel Company's general manager was informed that there was an emergency at Sangatte. He was sitting at the telex operator's desk firing questions at the duty manager at Sangatte just over half an hour after the explosion which had caused so much havoc.

1850 hrs. August 5th, The Tunnel Train

During the half hour there had been surprisingly little activity on the train. The handful of survivors of the first railway crash to take place under the English Channel were still too shocked to take any useful action. So shocked were they, in fact, that very little was said, let alone done, during those first thirty minutes.

Immediately after the crash the only passenger still sitting alone and in his own seat was the international squash player, Tambroni.

Alan Cannon, the computer firm manager, was the first to speak.

'Is anyone hurt?' he asked timidly. To his left he could just make out the outline of Peter Cater. In the darkness of the carriage nothing more was visible even at a distance of less than a metre.

'I think we're all right,' said Mr Black from somewhere in front of him.

'Yes, thank you,' said Louise.

Slowly the others confirmed that they were unhurt, although Tambroni complained that he had sprained a muscle in his left forearm. Susan Roberts answered for herself and Raenackers.

'Where do you think we are?' asked Dr Chatwyn.

'I can't see my watch,' said Dr Singh. 'Has anyone got the right time? A watch with a luminous dial?'

'It's 18.46,' said Alan Cannon.

'You're a minute fast,' said Peter Cater.

'We'll split the difference,' suggested Cannon, light-heartedly.

'OK!' said Cater.

'It's 18.45 and a half,' Cannon corrected himself.

'What time did we leave?' asked Dr Chatwyn.

'It was twenty minutes past six,' said Mrs Black unexpectedly. 'I saw the clock at the terminal.'

'We crashed about ten minutes ago,' said Dr Chatwyn, thinking aloud. 'So we'd been travelling for about fifteen minutes. How far do you think we travelled in fifteen minutes?'

'We're somewhere under the Channel,' said Gower flatly. 'The bloody thing's probably caved in.'

Louise Black screamed.

'That was a tactless thing to say,' complained her mother.

'We ought to get to know each other,' said Miss Millington. 'Introduce ourselves. So that we know who's talking.'

'That's a good idea,' said Mr Black. He introduced himself and the rest of his family.

'Where are you sitting?' asked Peter Cater.

'We're on the front row,' said Mrs Black.

'Let's take it by rows then,' suggested Cater.

'Right,' agreed Mr Black. 'Who's on the second row?' He turned round and peered into the blackness behind him.

'There are fourteen of us,' said David Black, who'd been counting, when the introductions were completed.

'Has anyone got a torch?' asked Peter Cater. 'It's a bit spooky sitting in the dark like this.'

'How stupid!' said Singh and Chatwyn together. They both reached inside their jacket pockets and brought out thin but powerful torches, the sort of pen-lights that doctors use to enable them to see when they peer down patient's throats. Ironically, the torches were presents from the manufacturers of Angipax.

'Just use one at a time in case the batteries run out," suggested Alan Cannon.

'These last for hours and hours,' Chatwyn reassured him.

'I'll put mine off for now,' agreed Singh, nevertheless, putting his torch back into his pocket.

Chatwyn stood up, holding on to the side of the seat in front of him and shone his torch into the different corners of the carriage. He picked out each face in turn.

When the light had moved away Louise whispered to her mother.

'Can't you wait a while?' asked her mother.

Louise shook her head, then, remembering that her mother could not see her, whispered to say that she could not.

'Is there a toilet anywhere?' Mrs Black asked.

No one answered.

'I don't think there is,' said Mrs Millington.

Louise started to cry.

'Can't you wait? demanded her father crossly.

'She can't,' said Mrs Black, defending her daughter.

'Have you got a plastic bag, dear?' asked Miss Millington quietly.

'Somewhere,' said Mrs Black.

'Well, it isn't an ideal solution but she'll feel more comfortable,' said Miss Millington. 'If we're stuck here much longer I'm sure we'll all have exactly the same problem quite soon.'

Mrs Black emptied a piece of Camembert cheese from a small plastic bag, and Louise Black, sobbing with shame and embarrassment, sat forward on the edge of her seat and urinated into the bag.

1852 hrs. August 5th, Montmartre, Paris

'Who found her?' asked Inspector Tissot.

'I did sir,' said a pink-faced young gendarme, standing, alert and neatly scrubbed, at the far end of the bedroom. Tissot noticed that he had the beginnings of a moustache and idly wondered how the youth expected anyone to take him seriously with the evidence of anticipated manhood so clearly visible.

Tissot said nothing for a moment. Then he moved forward slowly and stared down at the woman's body. 'Take her along to the morgue and get hold of Leboyer or Chandos or one of those damned doctors. We'd better have a post mortem done, but if whores are murdered, they're usually knifed or strangled.'

He turned away and marched out of the room, his shoes crunching on the dirty linoleum.

1854 hrs. August 5th, place Vendôme, Paris

After speaking to the duty manager at Sangatte, Garin rang the Heliport d'Issy les Moulineaux, which lies between the centre of Paris and St Quentin en Yvelines. He arranged for a helicopter to be ready and waiting for him within half an hour, able to take him north and prepared to wait for him at the tunnel terminal, ready if necessary to bring him back to Paris.

Ninety-five minutes later he was in Sangatte.

1900 hrs. August 5th, Sangatte Terminal

While Garin was preparing to leave Paris and fly to Sangatte, the duty terminal manager and the duty controller were desperately trying to find out what had happened. Forty minutes after the crash they still did not know why their screens were blank and why there had been such a total systems failure.

And so the duty manager had telephoned the resident engineer and his deputy as soon as he had spoken to Garin in Paris. The terminal organisation at Sangatte was far more complex and well-equipped than the organisation at Westernhanger. This was no reflection on the management at Westernhanger, but resulted from the political decision to base all the main management resources for the Tunnel in France. The safety officer and resident engineer at Sangatte were in fact responsible for the entire Tunnel and came directly under Garin's jurisdiction.

The resident engineer, Thomas Raspail, and his deputy Denis Bleriot, both lived in houses in the old village of Sangatte. The arrival of the terminal had inevitably brought with it a considerable need for new housing. The terminal staff consisted both of local inhabitants and experts brought in from other parts of France. Many of the Channel Tunnel Company's employees lived on a small housing estate which had been built to help accommodate them, but Raspail and Bleriot, both highly paid, lived, together with the three terminal managers, in older, more expensive houses in the village.

When telephoned by the duty manager, Raspail was playing badminton in the garden with his teenage daughter. Bleriot was in the bath while his wife prepared dinner for a small party of friends when his telephone call arrived. Both men muttered and moaned a little but both drove straight to the terminal some three miles distant.

'This is impossible,' insisted Raspail as he stared dismally at the row of blank screens in the control room, 'Quite impossible.'

Bleriot, who'd arrived a few minutes later in view of the fact that he'd needed to dry and clothe himself, shivered slightly. 'I wish it was,' he muttered, to himself as much as to Raspail.

It was Bleriot who arranged for a member of the maintenance crew to prepare a small work vehicle which was normally used to enable the workmen to inspect the tunnel. Raspail began trying to check the fire and ventilation control systems. The duty manager hurried off to try and placate the several hundred angry and impatient passengers who were collected in the terminal buildings and moaning about the delay.

While Louise Black sat sobbing, nursing an empty bladder and a full plastic bag, and Philippe Garin packed his small suitcase, Denis Bleriot and two members of his maintenance crew boarded the small open work-engine and set off for the tunnel entrance. Huge, powerful searchlights, fitted to the front of the engine, lit up the tunnel interior. A few minutes after entering the tunnel the three men noticed that the tracks along which they were travelling were almost submerged in thick soft clay. The driver of the work-engine slowed down and Bleriot jumped off the platform on to the floor of the tunnel. The clay squelched and Bleriot sank in to his ankles. He walked forward a few metres and the clay slowly began to move up to his calves.

The driver and the second maintenance man looked at each other.

'You'd better get back on board,' the driver said to Bleriot. He pointed forwards. The searchlights picked out the tunnel for several hundred metres ahead. The muddy clay could plainly be seen. Where they were, it was clearly no more than a few inches deep. In the distance they could see that the tunnel was filled with it.

'Merde,' said Bleriot softly.

'We'll have to get back now if we're going.' The driver warned. 'We'll be stuck in a minute or two.'

'Merde,' said Bleriot again. 'The bloody tunnel's collapsed.'

2029 hrs. August 5th, Sangatte, France

It was dark when Garin arrived at the control room in Sangatte. The helicopter landed in the car parking behind the control room. Warned by radio of Garin's approach the terminal manager had arranged for a landing area to be marked out with luminous cones. The last time the cones had been used had been at the opening ceremony when a number of dignitaries had arrived by helicopter.

'We've turned the conference room into an emergency centre,' shouted Martini as they hurried away from the helicopter. Behind them the pilot swung himself down from the helicopter and tried to arrange with two puzzled and confused mechanics for his machine to be refuelled.

Because it was used for training sessions and staff meetings one wall of the conference room was covered by a huge map of the entire tunnel complex, including the terminals at Sangatte and Westernhanger. Differently coloured lines drawn along the tunnel denoted the positions of ventilation shafts, electrical cables and television cameras. The map was made of a plastic material; and, alongside, fixed to the wall, there was a large box of coloured wax crayons which could be used to add new features to the map.

'Coffee?' said Bleriot, walking across to the percolator, plugged in and standing on a trolley which also carried several dozen cups and saucers.

The other three all nodded. Garin muttered genuine thanks. Bleriot poured out four black coffees, picked up the cups one by one and carried them over to the conference table. Roscoe carried over the milk jug and sugar bowl.

'From the silence I take it that the news isn't good,' said

Garin, wrapping his hands around his coffee cup and sipping at it cautiously.

'No,' said Bleriot bluntly. 'It isn't.' He got up and walked across to the map, hesitated for a moment with his fingers hovering over the box of crayons and then picked out a black crayon.

'We went in on the work engine,' he explained, drawing a thick black line down the middle of the tunnel. 'At about here there was clay lying on the track.' He drew a thick line at right angles to the tunnel. 'And we had to stop a few hundred metres further on, here,' he continued, drawing a second thick line at right angles to the tunnel.

Garin said nothing but stood up, put down his coffee and walked across to the map. He peered closely at the marks Bleriot had made.

'The tunnel looks to be blocked from about here,' said Bleriot, marking a third thick line across the tunnel.

'How far in is that?'

'About 12 kilometres,' said Bleriot.

'All clay?' asked Garin.

'As far as we can see,' Bleriot nodded.

'All the communications systems are out of order from here,' said Raspail, drawing a blue line next to Bleriot's third black line.

Garin still said nothing. He walked back to the table, picked up his coffee cup and sipped thoughtfully.

'I've made an announcement to the passengers we've got waiting,' said Roscoe. 'I've told them there's been a technical problem in the tunnel.'

'What about the press?' asked Garin. 'Does anyone outside this building know what's happened?'

'Not that I know of,' said Roscoe. 'But we haven't made a great secret of it. All the people working here know we've got real problems.'

'Then the press will be here soon,' said Garin. 'Send a telex to Paris and get them to send a press officer down here. We'll need someone to make statements, and keep journalists out of our hair.'

Roscoe left the room and went to send Garin's message.

'What's in the tunnel?' Garin asked Raspail, the safety officer.

'Three trains,' answered Raspail. 'Two passengers and one freight.'

'All in the England-bound tunnel?' asked Garin, astonished.

'No,' answered Raspail, quickly. 'One's in the other tunnel, about two miles out from the English coast.'

'Don't tell me that tunnel's blocked as well?' demanded Garin. 'I thought it was just the England-bound tunnel where we had the problem.'

'It is,' said Raspail. 'We stopped the other train when we realised we had a problem.'

'And you've left the bloody thing where it is?'

Raspail swallowed. 'We thought it would be safer than moving it until we knew exactly what was happening.'

Garin looked at his watch. 'It's nearly three hours since it happened,' he said. 'Three bloody hours and you've just left the damned thing where it is?'

Raspail said nothing.

'If there is a major fault, moving the train could be dangerous,' said Bleriot in their defence.

'Have you tried getting the passengers out of there?'

Bleriot shook his head.

'What are they doing at Westernhanger?'

'They're waiting for us to make a decision,' said Bleriot.

'Have they tried getting in at the other end of the England-bound tunnel?'

'The Westernhanger maintenance crew sent a remote control viewer in,' said Bleriot. 'The whole tunnel is blocked about four kilometres from the English exit.'

'Clay?'

Bleriot shook his head, 'Rock.'

'So pretty much the whole of the England-bound tunnel is blocked with rock, and God knows what else?'

'That's right,' said Raspail softly.

'And we have a freight train and a passenger train in the middle of it all?'

'That's right,' said Raspail. 'Roscoe's got the passenger lists.'

'We're getting the infrasound and the audio equipment set up at our end,' said Bleriot.

'How many passengers on the train out of Westernhanger?' asked Garin.

'One hundred and seventy-five,' replied Raspail.

'Get them out of there now,' said Garin. 'Send in anything but get them out. Leave the train where it is.'

2145 hrs. August 5th, The Tunnel Train

Inside the train it was hot and stuffy. Breathing was difficult and most of the passengers had discarded much of their clothing. The semi-hysterical arguments, proposals and accusations which had filled the first hour or so had died down. Now it was quiet and peaceful inside the compartment.

On the front row the Blacks were trying hard to reassure one another. To her own surprise, Mrs Black had turned out to be imbued with a surprising amount of spiritual strength. David Black, father of the family and reactionary enough still to consider himself responsible for their safety, had suffered two attacks of angina while waiting for the rescue he confidently expected. He had surreptitiously slipped several pills underneath his tongue at the onset of the first pains, and since then most of his energies had gone into fighting off the feeling of faintness and sickness which was threatening to overwhelm him.

Mrs Black felt really needed for the first time in ten years. At home they had all the usual domestic machinery, and, to satisfy her husband's social aspirations, they even had a cleaning woman. They couldn't really afford her and they didn't really need her, but David liked to be able to get his friends to ring him at home and leave messages with Mrs Fowler. The Black's pantry was stocked from top to bottom with packets and tins of ready-made meals that required nothing more imaginative than the addition of water or milk to turn them into food ready for the plate. Her life had become a series of coffee mornings, committee meetings and hospital library sessions now that the children were at school.

Here, stranded on the train, Mrs Black felt that her family needed her and she found the experience strangely satisfying.

Somehow she felt guilty about her own lack of concern or fear. She would never have been able to admit it, but Mrs Black was actually enjoying the experience. She felt closer to her husband than she had felt for years.

On the row behind the Blacks the two doctors were quietly discussing the atmospheric conditions within the carriage. Both men knew well that breathing was becoming more and more difficult and that the oxygen available within the carriage would inevitably run out before many more hours had elapsed. Dr Singh had a pocket calculator with a luminous console.

'How big do you think this place is?' asked Chatwyn.

'How many rows of seats are there?'

'Five,' replied Chatwyn after a moment's thought.

'With each seat taking up about a metre altogether?'

'I should think so.'

'Allow at most an extra metre for the thickness of the seats themselves.'

'I'd counted that within the metre.'

'Really?'

'It's about a metre from the back of our seat to the back of the seat in front,' whispered Chatwyn.

'OK. So five metres.'

'That's the length. What about the width?'

'It's not more than half a metre per seat,' said Singh.

'Say three metres in width?'

Singh nodded. Chatwyn took his silence for agreement.

'And when we came in I had to bend my head. Allow an extra half-metre for the space above the door. That's about two and a half metres high.'

'So the volume is five times three times two and a half cubic metres?' said Chatwyn. Singh pressed the appropriate buttons. The green numbers lit up as he did so.

'Thirty seven and a half cubic metres,' said Singh.

'How many litres of air are there in a cubic metre?' asked Chatwyn.

'God knows,' said Singh. He took out his diary, switched on his pocket torch and studied the pages at the front. 'I've never even looked at all this rubbish,' he muttered. 'I've always wondered why the hell they put it in diaries.'

'Obviously for people trapped in tunnels,' said Chatwyn, drily.

Singh flicked over several pages before finding the one he wanted. 'There are a thousand litres in a cubic metre,' he announced finally with some astonishment. To save the batteries he turned off his torch.

'So we've got 37,500 litres of air?'

'That's right.'

'How many litres of oxygen in that?'

'Air contains about 21% oxygen.'

'So we've got about 7,500 litres of oxygen.'

'Exactly.'

'How long will that last us?'

'The working man uses up about 2,000 litres of air an hour. At rest he'll get by with a twentieth of that.'

'About 400 litres of oxygen an hour down to 20 litres an hour.'

'And we've got 7,500.'

'How many of us are there?'

'Fourteen,' said Chatwyn.

'That's about 536 litres of oxygen each,' said Singh, operating the calculator again.

'Say 500.'

'OK.'

'We've been in here for about two hours,' said Chatwyn very quietly.

'So if we all keep very still we've got at most another 23 hours.'

'At the very most,' agreed Chatwyn.

'That assumes we can use up every scrap of oxygen in the air we've got.'

'It would get very nasty long before then.'

'We'd be unconscious.'

'How long do you think before we go unconscious?'

'I don't know,' said Singh, shaking his head.

'We'll have to get out of this compartment.'

'You go across to the far seat,' suggested Singh. 'I'll take a look at the wall on my side. Perhaps we can find a way out.'

'There's no door,' said Chatwyn. 'I remember reading in a brochure they handed us that none of the compartments have doors or windows. It's a security measure to stop people throwing bombs out into the tunnel.'

'There must be some way out of this tin can,' said Singh.

'It isn't tin,' corrected Chatwyn. 'The damned thing is mostly plastic.'

'We'll have a look at it anyway,' said Singh. He turned away and began to examine the carriage wall next to his seat.

* * *

The five passengers on the middle row of compartment 22 were silent. Alan Cannon was thinking of the dead woman he'd left behind in Paris. He had never paid much attention to religious dogma but it seemed to him that he was being punished. If the punishment would expiate his sins he would gladly accept it. For years he had been straddling the line between sanity and insanity. Now he felt himself slipping to one side; under pressure as a result of the death of the Montmartre whore, and his incarceration in the train, Cannon was close to cracking. Somehow he felt removed from the other passengers. He saw his role as simple and practical. It was his task to lead these other people out of danger.

* * *

Peter Cater was conscious of almost every second that ticked by. He could not help thinking of the bizarre and almost insignificant events which could have prevented his involvement in the disaster. If he had missed the train. If he'd broken his leg in Paris. If he'd been arrested for importing pornography. If one of the children had been ill he wouldn't have left home at all. There were a million 'ifs' and no reasons. It was all so much of a waste, all so undeniably stupid.

He fingered the two coins which he had taken from his jacket pocket. They reminded him of the photographs he'd sold to Luillard. They both comforted him and alarmed him. The coins, together with the others he had stored in an empty tin in the garden shed at home, represented future freedom from intellectual imprisonment. But they also reminded him of the world into which he had strayed almost accidentally. A world of exploitation and immense rewards, in which the greedy all too often used the simple-minded to satisfy the perverted. Cater thought of his own wife and their children. None of them suspected that he was involved in this other world. What would be their reactions if they did find out? His wife, for all her liberal attitudes, would be shocked and humiliated. Cater recognised the weaknesses of others only too well; he had too many of his own.

And was it only the money which led him to the pornography? He had suspected for a long time that there was more to it than that. He had undeniably derived considerable pleasure from his adventures with Felicity.

What if he were to die now? What would he have left behind in the world? A family which would survive very well without him, a small company which would probably collapse or be swallowed by one of the publishing giants, with Hugo accepting a position with a comfortable pension and a company car, and a few hundred photographs of a woman enjoying fornication, sodomy, fellatio and cunnilingus with feigned relish. What a legacy to leave as a permanent epitaph!

Angrily and impulsively Cater threw the two Roman coins away from him into the darkness. He heard them hit the far wall of the compartment and fall down on the floor. Then he buried his head in his hands and wept silently and fiercely.

* * *

Miss Millington wasn't thinking of anything much at all. She had enjoyed her trip south. The journey to Greece had been pleasant and eventful. She had met plenty of kind and thoughtful people. For herself she had no regrets. She really didn't mind if she never got back to England again at all. Going home would only be a serious of anticlimaxes, meetings in the church hall, shopping at the local supermarket, collecting her pension at the post office. The future held no great hopes for her. No, that wasn't true; the future held no hopes at all. Miss Millington was not at all afraid of dying. In fact, she was ready for it. In some ways Miss Millington was the strongest of them all. She had only her memories of the past to lose and nothing could eradicate those.

* * *

James Gower and Hélène Albric were both conscious that their affair was over. It wasn't anything that either of them had said. They both just knew it. And now they found each other's company an embarrassment. They both wanted to be out of it all and away from each other. Neither of them could explain just why it was all over. Perhaps it was the proximity to death that gave them some extra insight into their own lives. James Gower knew that he did not love Hélène; nor did he want to spend the rest of his life with her. He found her attractive and he had enjoyed his affair with her. He recognised that. He wouldn't change any of it. But his affair had contained no love. No, that wasn't right. There had been love. He really had loved her. The problem had been that he just hadn't liked her. They had never really had anything in common except the gallery and that just wasn't enough. When he got back to England he'd find some way to sack her. He'd give her some money and make sure that she didn't lose out financially.

Hélène had, however, already decided that if they ever saw England again she would resign from the gallery. She'd never realised before that her relationship with Gower had been based on all the wrong foundations. She'd admired his knowledge, enjoyed knowing that she was taking him from his wife, and enjoyed his physical presence. He was a good lover. But it wasn't enough. There was nothing more. She didn't believe in him or anything he stood for. She didn't know what he stood for. Nothing, probably. She enjoyed the material benefits of being his mistress but that was all. She shared nothing secret with him. Now that they were sitting in a compartment under the sea she had absolutely nothing to say to him. There was nothing they could talk about. It was all so much froth and so insubstantial. She wanted more out of life.

* * *

On the row behind them Benito Tambroni sat nursing his wrist. He knew that the injury was serious; just about as serious as it could be. He hated any sort of injury, for he despised the weak and infirm. And what was it all for? Some wretched tournament in some damned insignificant sports hall in some dreary part of England, where he would have been matched against a series of incompetent amateurs anxious to show that they could take points off a former world champion.

Tambroni hadn't always been bitter and unhappy. As a young champion he'd always been kind and generous. Always ready to sign a boy's autograph book. Always happy to have his photograph taken with a couple of fans. Even willing to turn up at charity functions for no fee at all. As the years went by, however, and he found himself playing against the same sort of dull insipid competition year after year, he began to hate the game and himself. And now the game was trying to kill him. If it hadn't been for the tournament in England he wouldn't have been on the train at all. It was all quite typical, Tambroni decided, quite typical of the luck he was having.

* * *

Susan Roberts and Gaston Raenackers weren't speaking to each other. For a while Raenackers had buried his head in his mistress's breast. Then Susan Roberts began to tire of his wretchedness and his snivelling. She herself felt naked and vulnerable. She knew that everyone thought of her as being competent and efficient, but just for once she wanted to be feminine, incompetent and dependent. Why couldn't she have a real man upon whose chest she could rest her head for a change? Raenackers, she decided, was hardly a man at all. Just a sex object to be discarded. Not what she really wanted.

2215 hrs. August 5th, Sangatte, France

Raspail was having trouble persuading the manager at Westernhanger to do anything at all.

'This really isn't the sort of decision I can take,' complained the Englishman.

'I'm not asking you to take any decisions,' explained Raspail. 'Simply do as I ask. I'm working under the authority of Philippe Garin.'

'My orders come from London,' argued the Westernhanger

manager. 'We have a procedure for policy-making decisions.'

'Listen to me very carefully,' said Raspail, his patience exhausted. 'Three double-engined, reversible hovercraft which can be driven into the tunnel on one engine and back out again on the other are on their way to you already from an excursion firm in Calais. They'll be nearly across the Channel by now. When they arrive I want you in the lavatory or screwing your secretary or somewhere quite unavailable. Those hovercraft are going to fly straight into your tunnel and they're picking up those passengers. If you don't want to take the decision to let them in, that's your business; but if you stop them flying in, you've got to make another decision and on the strength of that decision you could have a lot of blood on your hands. I'll make damned sure that everyone knows who was responsible for preventing the rescue.'

'Now wait a minute...,' began the manager indignantly.

'No. You wait. You just bloody well do as I've told you to do,' snapped an angry Raspail. He put down the telephone, wiped sweat from his forehead, and slumped back into his chair, eyes closed. It was hard to believe that just an hour or two earlier he'd been at home playing badminton in the garden.

2220 hrs. August 5th, Police Station, Montmartre, Paris

'Telephone call for you, Inspector,' called the young gendarme, holding one hand over the telephone mouthpiece and waving with his other hand to attract the inspector's attention.

'It's Dr Leboyer from the morgue,' the constable explained when the Inspector turned wearily from the coffee-vending machine and stared in his direction.

'That woman you found in Montmartre, the old tart, said Leboyer. 'You wanted a post mortem done on her quickly, remember?'

'I remember, doctor,' nodded Inspector Tissot. 'Have you got anything exciting for me?'

'Nothing you'll find exciting. She died a natural death; heart attack. She had the worst coronary arteries I've seen in a woman for years.'

'Nothing else?'

'Nothing at all to interest you,' said Leboyer with a laugh. 'She'd got fibroids, varicose veins and piles and an early cancer in her large bowel. She wasn't what I'd call a good insurance risk.' He laughed dryly, and put the telephone down.

'That's that then,' said Tissot to no one in particular. He crossed to the newly made up file which bore the dead woman's name, scrawled across the cover and threw it into an overflowing filing basket. The case was officially closed.

2230 hrs. August 5th, The Tunnel Train

The walls of compartment 22 were smooth plastic. There were no doors, no windows and no apparent weaknesses. Dr Chatwyn and Dr Singh met again when Dr Chatwyn shuffled across the compartment back to his original seat.

'We'll have to cut our way out,' whispered Chatwyn. He had mopped up moisture from the inside of the compartment wall with his shirt and was squeezing the resultant few drops of moisture into his mouth.

Singh agreed; he lit his pocket torch, stood up and shone the beam on to his own face. He spoke clearly so that everyone could hear him.

'Dr Chatwyn and I have been discussing our immediate plight and we feel that we need to make some sort of ventilation hole in the compartment wall.'

'What are we going to make a hole with?' asked James Gower. 'Surely we would be better off staying here. We'll be rescued soon enough.'

'We don't know what's outside,' pointed out David Black. 'We might be surrounded by water. If the tunnel roof has given in, we could have the English Channel out there. If you make a hole in the wall, water could come pouring in.'

Hélène Albric gasped audibly. Louise Black, who had stopped crying, started again.

'Really, David,' said Mrs Black sharply. 'Do you have to be so tactless?'

'If we don't make some sort of ventilation hole,' explained

Dr Singh patiently, 'we'll run out of air. This compartment is airtight and we're using up the oxygen we've got. I don't think we can afford to just sit and wait for much longer.'

'I agree entirely with Dr Singh,' said Chatwyn. 'I think we ought to do something.'

'I think we should get some ventilation and even try to get out of this damned compartment,' said Alan Cannon.

'I agree,' said Peter Cater.

'I'm always in favour of doing something,' said Miss Millington. She could not remember ever having such control over her destiny before.

'We should make the hole,' said Tambroni.

Having decided to puncture the compartment wall, the next problem was a more practical one; just how to do it.

'Has anyone got a knife?' asked Dr Chatwyn.

'I've got a pocket knife,' said James Black. He took out a scout's knife, the sort of weapon which contains a multitude of blades designed to enable Boy Scouts to remove stones from horses' hooves.

'We need something stronger than that, I'm afraid,' said Alan Cannon, who'd been investigating the compartment wall while the others had been arguing.

They all rummaged through their pockets. Tambroni had a small penknife, too, but that was even flimsier than the one James Black had produced. The most promising looking tool was as tin opener that Mrs Black produced from the bottom of her shopping bag.

'How the hell are you going to make a hole in the wall of a railway carriage with a tin opener?' demanded David Black. 'I've never heard anything so ludicrous in all my life.'

'We could probably make some sort of hole with it if we had something to hammer it in with,' said Dr Singh. He'd been banging ineffectively at the tin opener with his closed fist.

Again the others hunted around looking for something to use as a hammer. Towards the back of the compartment, Benito Tambroni silently picked up his elongated leather and canvas sports bag. He unfastened the three leather buckles at the front of the bag and took out one of the metal-rimmed squash rackets he carried with him. Tenderly, almost lovingly, he caressed the racket. It seemed sacrilegious to use it for so profane a purpose as hammering a tin opener into the plastic wall of a railway carriage. Still...

'Let's try this,' he said suddenly. He levered himself across and over the intervening seats to the spot where Dr Singh had been hammering at the compartment wall. There was a small depression in the plastic where the point of the tin opener had marked the surface.

'Let me try,' Tambroni said. He took the tin opener from Dr Singh, turned the racket so that the metal edge faced the opener and using the racket as a hammer gave the tin opener half a dozen quick, sharp blows. He moved so quickly that Dr Singh did not even have time to direct the beam of their remaining torch on to the tin opener.

Within three or four minutes Tambroni had hammered the tin opener into the wall to a depth of three millimetres.

'How thick do you think this damned wall is?' he asked of no one in particular.

'I should think you're through,' said Dr Singh, examining the wall with his torch.

'Then let's make the hole a bit bigger,' said Tambroni. He hammered at the side of the opener, first from the left and then from the right. The pain in his wrist was agonising.

'Hey, don't make it bigger yet,' complained James Gower. 'Let's see if water comes through first.'

Tambroni ignored him. Moments later he pulled the tin opener out of the compartment wall, grabbed the torch from Singh's hand and shone it directly into the hole. There was nothing but blackness but on his hand Tambroni could feel a stream of cool air under pressure.

'It's air!' he shouted. 'There's no water.'

Inside the compartment there was a cheer. Miss Millington clasped her hands together and smiled at nothing and no one in particular. She knew it couldn't end just yet.

2242 hrs. August 5th, Sangatte, France

Philippe Garin had enough problems. Bleriot had returned from the investigation of the England-bound tunnel with the news that the tunnel was apparently impenetrable,. The press officer in Paris had eventually been traced and ordered to organise a non-committal press conference, but already someone had leaked the news to a television company, and a camera crew and reporter had arrived on the spot. So far they'd been limited to interviewing some of the stranded and impatient passengers in the terminal but Garin knew that they wouldn't be satisfied with that for long. And as if that was not enough, Garin now had political pressures to contend with.

Claude Louis Noiret had telephoned Garin at the Sangatte terminal at twenty-five minutes past nine that evening.

'I rang your apartment and then the Paris office,' he explained. 'They told me I could get hold of you there. What the devil is going on?'

'I'm sorry you had so much difficulty,' apologised Garin, wondering what Noiret knew and who had told him.

'A friend of mine from the Foreign Ministry, a very highly placed official, has been on the telephone to me,' said Noiret, without waiting for any reply. 'He was on his way to England with his family and they're stranded at Sangatte. They've apparently been sitting in their car waiting for some sort of explanation for hours.'

'There's been an accident,' explained Garin, gingerly. 'A collapse of some sort.'

There was a silence from the other end.

'Are you still there?' asked Garin.

'I'm still here,' said Noiret. 'What do you mean – a collapse?'

'We're still trying to find out what happened,' said Garin. 'The tunnel is blocked. There's a passenger train in there. We haven't been able to get to the passengers.'

'A collapse?' replied Noiret. 'How could there be a collapse?'

'I don't know yet,' said Garin.

'Are you sure about this?'

'I'm afraid so.'

'Why wasn't I told?'

'There didn't seem a great deal of point in bothering the board members at this time of night,' said Garin. 'We're doing everything we can.'

'Do the press know?'

'If they don't they soon will.'

'I think you have badly mishandled this affair,' said Noiret stiffly. 'Your first duty lies to the board. I should have been informed. Do you expect me to wait until I read about it in the papers to hear that the tunnel has collapsed?' Noiret had raised his voice. Towards the end of the sentence he was almost shouting.

'I'm sorry,' said Garin.

'Sorry!' said Noiret. 'Who was on the train?'

'Who?'

'Were there any dignitaries on the train? Any politicians? Anyone important?'

'Not that I know of.'

'This is dreadful. Absolutely dreadful,' muttered Noiret.

'We shall have to call an emergency meeting of the board. We shall meet tomorrow.'

'Do you want me to see to it that the other board members are informed?' asked Garin.

'Yes. And I want you there personally,' said Noiret. I want an up-to-date report on the situation at Sangatte.' Garin's protests met with silence. Noiret had put the telephone down.

* * *

Fifteen minutes later Garin was speaking to Janine Boysee, the company's Marketing Director.

Garin explained briefly what had happened.

'Would you like me to get in touch with the other board members?' asked Janine Boysee.

'If you would,' said Garin gratefully. 'Apologise to them on my behalf for not getting in touch with them sooner, but explain that I've been trying to get the poor devils who are trapped in the tunnel out alive.'

'Do you think there are any survivors?' asked Madame Boysee.

'I have to assume that there are,' said Garin. 'Though if there is anyone trapped in there I don't know how long they can survive.'

'Good luck,' said Janine Boysee softly.

2302 hrs. August 5th, Zürich, Switzerland

News of the disaster in the Channel tunnel reached Herr Bruckner in Zürich shortly after it was broadcast on French television, reaching his elegant lakeside house automatically on the telex machine which was installed in his study. Not realising that Susan Roberts was on the train which was trapped, and not knowing that his firm's supply of ingredients for Angipax had been responsible for a large part of the explosion which had caused the disaster, Bruckner simply dropped the tape into a shredder which he kept next to the tape machine, and went to bed.

Dr Jackson, however, did know that the chemicals for the manufacture of Angipax were on the train leaving Sangatte for England at approximately 18.00 the previous evening. When he heard of the crash through a telephone call from an assistant at the Zürich offices, he immediately realised the significance of it. He telephoned Sangatte, confirmed that his firm's consignment had been on the trapped train, and drove straight back into the city from his villa just outside it. When he arrived in his office, he telephoned Jean Seno at St Quentin, and arranged for a substitute supply of erythrytyl tetranitrate and petanerythritol tetranitrate to be shipped by road to Calais and then taken across the Channel by specially chartered ferry.

Being a thorough and careful businessman, Dr Jackson then telephoned the European Credit Bank in Luxembourg and asked them to check whether or not Miss Roberts had arrived safely in England. They rang him back ten minutes later to tell him that Miss Roberts appeared to be on the train which was trapped in the tunnel.

They assured him, however, that there was no need for concern. A substitute for Miss Roberts, a Dr Thaier, had already been recalled from Vienna and would be flying to London directly. Briefing documents would meet him in London and the deal with the British car firm would go through as planned. Any potential inconvenience to ACR Drogues et Cie had been avoided.

Satisfied that all was well, Dr Jackson left his office, gave instructions that he was to be called again in case of any further emergency, and drove back to his villa where he drank one small glass of rather good brandy before going to bed quite alone.

PART THREE

0005 hrs. August 6th, Nottingham, England

Mrs Cater's mother had arrived and was making another pot of tea. The children were all in bed and fast asleep; Mrs Cater's father had made numerous additional telephone calls to the emergency number. There was still no information about Peter.

Julie had wanted to drive to Westernhanger, to the tunnel terminal, but her mother had stopped her.

'What can you do?' she asked. 'You're better off here. As soon as there is any news, we'll drive you down there.'

So they sat and waited.

* * *

It was unbearably hot inside the train. Most of the passengers had stripped to their underwear. Singh and Tambroni had been working at the thick green plastic wall of compartment 22 for what seemed like hours. Using Tambroni's squash racket they'd hammered the tin opener through the wall more than a dozen times, making a small ring of holes about the size of a man's hand.

'Wait a moment,' said Tambroni, taking the racket from Dr Singh when the ring of holes was completed. 'Let's try and knock that centre piece out now.'

All four of the passengers who had been near the spot where they'd concentrated their effort had noticed that powerful streams of air had been pouring through the small holes they had made. They had all assumed that the air outside the compartment had been under greater pressure than the air inside the compartment. It had not been a discovery any of them had found either heartening or worrying. It was enough for them to know that it was air and not water outside their trapped compartment.

None of them was prepared for what happened next. The ring of plastic which they had been trying to cut out of the wall was being hammered outwards by Tambroni. But that did not stop it flying inwards when it finally came loose and broke free from the rest of the wall. Tambroni, who might have expected to find his squash racket handle flying forwards, out of the compartment, instead found it being forced backwards. And the irregular, sharp-edged disc of heavy plastic flew inwards, into the compartment with horrific force. It sliced through Tambroni's right wrist and hit Dr Singh just above his cricoid cartilage. It stopped only when it crashed against the anterior side of Dr Singh's cervical spine.

No one had much of an idea what had happened. Dr Chatwyn's torch had been blasted out of his hand by the stream of air which rushed into the compartment and they were all immediately plunged into unrelieved darkness. Most of the people in the compartment were immediately sprayed with a shower of blood from both Singh and Tambroni, and since, in the dark one fluid feels very much like another, nearly all of them were convinced immediately that they were about to be drowned.

The result was that for the second time since they had all been trapped together, the passengers in compartment 22 panicked quite completely.

The panic was accentuated by the fact that as the air from outside the compartment continued to rush into the compartment, it whipped up everything light inside and whirled it around and around. Clothes, odd bits of paper, fragments of food and Dr Singh's blood circled round and round their heads. The blood, whipped into a fine spray as it spurted from his severed arteries, kept them all convinced that they were about to drown. James Gower screamed that the water had reached his knees and tried to stand up on his seat. Hélène Albric, to her own surprise, found herself perhaps cooler and calmer than anyone. She listened to James Gower's screams of anguish, knew very well that the carriage was not being flooded with water, and realised that she despised him. Benito Tambroni could not understand why his right hand seemed to have lost all power. With his left hand he explored first his arm and then the immobile hand. He did so calmly, less excited by the events of the last few moments than anyone else in the compartment.

It was Hélène Albric who realised that the fluid falling on her was not water but blood. Trying to brush away a few drops that had fallen on her face, she noticed how sticky and gelatinous they were. She thought that perhaps it was mud rather than water and held her fingers, which she had used to brush away the fluid, to her nose and sniffed. The she licked tentatively at her fingers.

'It's blood!' she whispered in horror, to herself more than anyone else. At first no one heard her. 'It's blood,' she shouted, her newly found calm evaporating.

Her words stilled her fellow travellers.

'It's not water, it's blood,' shouted Hélène again. 'Taste it.'

In the dark, twelve fingers were rubbed tentatively in the places were the falling fluid had landed on skin, and then those twelve fingers were slipped gingerly between twenty four lips.

'Someone's been cut,' said Dr Chatwyn. 'Don't panic.'

He felt himself panicking and his words were intended as much to calm himself as to calm the others. What if he had to cope with a real injury? It was years since he'd even seen blood. Then it had been his own. What did you do to stop bleeding? A tourniquet? No, that was old-fashioned, these days you just applied pressure. Simply pressed on the bleeding site until the blood clotted. Then what? And in the dark! Perhaps, he thought, perhaps Dr Singh knows more about these things. He turned to where his companion should have been, reached across for him and found his fingers sliding across a blood-soaked chest. He withdrew his fingers in horror.

'I've lost the torch,' he whispered hoarsely. 'Look for the torch.'

The others reached instinctively for the floor, scrabbling for Dr Chatwyn's torch. Miss Millington found it eventually. It had fallen on to the seat beside her. She fiddled with the switch but could not make it work. She passed it forwards, whispering: 'Here, here!' to guide Chatwyn's fingers to it.

The torch was broken. The bulb and glass had been smashed. Chatwyn remembered his own torch, which had died an hour earlier. He took it out of his pocket, emptied the useless batteries out of it, and replaced them with the batteries from Dr Singh's broken torch.

Then he switched it on. By sheer accident the beam of the torch when it came on was aimed directly at Dr Singh's head. Dr Singh was lying back across two of the seats, with his head hanging over the back of one seat, and the gaping hole in his neck made all the more obvious for that fact. Blood still spurted and bubbled out of the severed vessels. The plastic disc was still half-embedded in flesh. Mrs Black fainted, James Gower was sick and Gaston Raenackers lost control of his bowels. At that moment Tambroni discovered why it was that he had no strength at all in his right hand.

0135 hrs. August 6th Sangatte, France

Although it seemed much longer, it was seven hours since the explosion. News of the crash had been broadcast on the late programmes of all European Television networks. The reports had included an interview with Claude Louis Noiret, who spoke confidently and brightly about hopes for the trapped passengers. It had been, he said with all the assurance of a man with no facts at all to impede him, a natural disaster which no planning could have foreseen. It had been a unique and unfortunate setback, he admitted, but he was certain that the tunnel would soon be in operation once more. Moreover, he pointed out, the number of people who had travelled through the tunnel was already to be counted in hundreds of thousands, and an accident involving a small number of people was unfortunately a statistical inevitably.

This last statement, intended to allay fears and soften the news, proved disastrous. The President of the French Travellers' Association, a consumer pressure group formed to try to influence the activities of all forms of organisation concerned with the transport and accommodation of travellers, issued a press statement in which he deplored the attitude of M. Noiret.

It looked as if a major row was brewing; and anxious, as ever, for the full story, the international press sent teams of reporters and photographers to Sangatte. By midnight, there were no less than thirteen television crews camped in the car park outside the control room, and every hotel in Sangatte had received telephone calls and cables from journalists requiring rooms. One American news magazine hired an aeroplane to fly a team of six reporters and photographers across the Atlantic, and it was rumoured that a television company had hired a submarine fitted with facilities for filming underwater.

It was with this as the background that a meeting of all the Channel Tunnel Company's experts began at thirty-five minutes past one in the morning.

'We can begin with some good news,' said Raspail when they'd all settled. He didn't wait for Garin to give him permission to speak. They all recognised that there were far more important things to worry about than formality or protocol.

The other six pairs of eyes turned towards him.

'I've just heard from Westernhanger,' said Raspail.

'They've managed to get all the passengers off the France-bound train. There were no real problems and no casualties. The only snag seems to be that the manager there has reported to London that I was rude and aggressive.' He shrugged and a half-smile appeared on his face. It might have been a defensive half-smile, but Garin nodded his general approval and the smile broadened.

'Do we know where the train is yet? asked Garin.

'We've got it more or less pinpointed,' said Bleriot.

'The total distance between Sangatte and Westernhanger is about 64 kilometres. The tunnel, of course, is 48 kilometres long and the distance from the terminal here is about the same as the distance in England – something like 8 kilometres. The tunnel runs underground for 7 kilometres on our side of the Channel before it goes underneath the Channel itself. On the English side, there are 5 kilometres of tunnel underground but not underneath the sea.'

No one spoke but they all watched Bleriot as he studied his notes.

'Use the map,' suggested Martini.

'Right,' said Bleriot. He stood and moved swiftly across the huge plan of the tunnel.

'We think the freight train is stuck approximately here,' said Bleriot, pointing on the map. 'About 20 kilometres into the tunnel. The passenger train is almost directly behind it.'

'If we can get some infrasound equipment in there,' said Garin, 'we could find out just where the train is.'

'What's it like from the English side?' asked Bleriot.

'The English-bound tunnel?'

Bleriot nodded.

'I've got one of the hovercraft crews who took off the passengers from the France-bound train to check it out,' said Raspail. He looked at his watch. 'I should hear from them fairly soon.'

'Do we know what caused the collapse?' asked Garin.

Bleriot shrugged his shoulders. 'No idea.'

'No suggestion it was deliberate?'

'None,' said Bleriot. 'How would anyone blow it up? The security is meticulous.'

'What about natural causes?' asked Garin.

'No,' said Raspail. 'I don't think so. Definitely not.' He shook his head wearily to emphasise the denial.

'Why are you so sure?'

'We've been in touch with seismological centres in both Paris and London,' said Raspail. 'I spoke to people in both centres.'

'What about a natural gas pocket?'

'No.' said Bleriot. 'Our surveys would have shown one if there was one there.'

'So we're back where we started?' said Garin.

'I suppose it could have been an industrial cargo,' said Raspail. 'Some freight that blew up.'

'We don't carry explosives,' said Martini. 'All freight is carefully checked.'

'Can you get us a list?' asked Garin. 'I'd like to see the freight manifest. With a breakdown.'

'Certainly,' said Martini. 'It'll take me ten minutes.'

'Why don't we have a fifteen minute break?' suggested Garin.

'I'd like the freight manifest,' he began, looking at Martini and holding up one finger of his left hand. 'Some idea of what it's like in the tunnel on the English side of the trapped train.' A second finger. 'Some idea of when we can get an infrasound report from this side if we can get a hovercraft in there on top of the mud.' A third finger. 'I'd like another fifty volunteers to be on call,' he said, looking at Harnaud, the other duty manager. 'Finally,' he added, holding up his thumb. 'I'd like a press release ready. I'll have to make some sort of statement to the press.' He sighed. 'Fifteen minutes, gentlemen,' he said. He stood up and headed for the door. He felt very, very tired. He turned. 'And if anyone has any bright ideas about how we're going to get in there and get the passengers out, I'd love to hear them,' he added.

* * *

They met again fifteen minutes later. Martini had arranged for a huge plateful of steaming hot croissants to be put on the table together with a pile of plates and linen napkins., The percolator bubbled cheerfully with a fresh supply of coffee.

'Right,' said Garin. 'Let's get on with it. 'He picked a croissant from the pile and dug a knife into a potful of English marmalade. His face was showing signs of the strain and tension under which he had been working for the last six hours or so.

He turned to Martini. 'Have you got that freight manifest?'

Martini nodded, picked up a piece of yellow paper from the table in front of him and began to read from it.

'Thirty tons of fruit, twenty-five tons of tea, spare parts for Renault cars, mainly exhaust pipes and radiators, 15,000 motor car tyres, 25,000 copies of each of three EEC publications on import/export regulations in English, French and German; materials for the manufacture of a heart drug being sold under the trade name of Angipax, 15,000 plastic dolls, sixteen tons of washing machine motors and two hundred racing cycles. That's it.' He put the piece of paper back down on the table in front of him and sat back. He threw out his arms. 'I can't see anything there that could cause an explosion,' he said. 'All these manifests have to be double checked. I'd stake my job on the fact that nothing has been switched or added.'

'You have no choice about that,' said Garin bluntly. 'If someone has been switching cargoes and sending explosives through the tunnel we can all start reading the situations vacant advertisements.'

This stark warning was greeted with silence.

'Anyone got any bright ideas about getting into that train?' asked Garin.

'What about drilling down through the sea bed?' suggested Martini.

Bleriot shook his head. 'We'd get into the tunnel,' he agreed. 'But we don't know whether there are any survivors, if there are any. The chances of us hitting the right part of the tunnel are infinitesimal. And there's the real risk that when we break through, the tunnel would collapse even more. Then we'd just stand a chance of killing off anyone who's left.' He shook his head sadly.

'If we're going to get anyone out,' said Bleriot. 'It'll be through the connecting tunnels.'

'I agree,' said Garin. 'Concentrate on those. If we can get into the pilot tunnel and then find a connecting tunnel that gets us from the pilot tunnel into the main England-bound tunnel, we'll at least have some sort of idea of whether there is anyone alive in there.' He stood up. 'I'll join you in twenty minutes,' he promised. He turned to the press officer, 'Have you got that release ready?'

0300 hrs. August 6th, The Tunnel Train

It is not easy to forget how close death may be when there is an exsanguinated human body within touching distance. And when that body's blood is spread over everything in your world then it is painfully clear just how close death is. Dr Chatwyn had switched off his pocket torch within seconds of identifying the body of his former companion. There was no mystery about the death, no need to investigate for signs of life and no one expected Chatwyn to be able to do anything to restore Dr Singh to the living. Slowly, as the pressure inside the compartment began to equal the pressure outside the tunnel, the whirling miscellany of aerial flotsam began to subside. Papers and clothes slowly descended – arbitrarily, so that the scarf which Peter Cater had bought his wife ended up at Louise Black's feet and Miss Millington's cardigan ended up on an empty seat next to Susan Roberts.

Compartment 22 had been trapped in a short section of tunnel with rock and mud sealing off the tunnel in both directions. About fifty metres of tunnel roof had held and remained in place. In front of compartment 22, the other compartments and the freight train were smashed and crushed unrecognisably. Only the last compartment – 22 – was relatively undamaged although even it has been knocked on to one side so that it leant crazily against the tunnel wall. It was through the wall which was leaning towards the tunnel door that Tambroni and Singh had made their small air vent. The pressure of the trapped air, caught between the tunnel walls and the mud and rock which had fallen in both directions, had been quite enough to cause Dr Singh's death and Benito Tambroni's injury.

Behind compartment 22, in the direction from which they had come, the tunnel was blocked by a massive roof fall which had been caused by the blast from the freight train explosion. The blast had somehow left compartment 22 untouched and gone on to destroy several hundred metres of tunnel roof, allowing clay to fall through into the tunnel.

To understand why this should have happened it is necessary to understand that the cross-Channel tunnel did not simply go down to a certain depth, go under the Channel and then come up again. When the route for the tunnel had been planned, the investigating engineers had gone to a great deal of trouble to measure the strength of the rock through which they were tunnelling, and the depth of the sea above. For the floor of the channel is more like a mountain range than a swimming pool bottom. There are valleys as well as mountains, small hills and minor depressions. And, just as in any stretch of land, there are weaknesses and breaks, gulleys and hollows.

When the tunnel had been built it had been designed to avoid weak spots, to go round dangerous areas where extra pressures might be exerted on the tunnel roof or walls, and to go through the most suitable sort of rock. Inevitably, therefore, the tunnel sometimes went up on a slight incline and sometimes went down. The trains sometimes had to climb and sometimes descend.

About a quarter of a kilometre behind the rear portion of the passenger train, in other words the trailing end of compartment 22, the tunnel roof had been opened by the repair engineers who had been attending to wiring faults. The engineers had already abandoned their work for the day when the explosion occurred, but they had left the panels which sealed off the roof out of position. The panels served merely to hide and protect the electrical systems within the roof and since there was no chance at all of any passenger catching a glimpse of the missing roof panels, the fact that they were left propped up on the metal catwalk seemed of little significance to the repair crew. It was, however, crucial to the passengers trapped in compartment 22. When the blast from the explosion reached the open part of the roof it happened to be getting to the bottom of a slight incline. The air rushed into the ceiling compartment and immediately ripped off several dozen other ceiling panels further along the line. With the panels, the blast tore away all the electrical wiring and air conditioning equipment. It also triggered off the automatic sprinkler devices, designed to come into operation in the event of a fire. There was now no fire, but the finely adjusted valves which would have allowed water to come through if heat had melted their sealing mechanisms, simply disappeared; they were snapped off and blown down the tunnel.

The explosive blast had also ripped two metal segments out of the tunnel roof. With those two segments, several thousand tons of loose clay had fallen into the tunnel. In terms of the total amount of rock and earth which lay on top of the tunnel roof, the amount which fell in was relatively insignificant. It was, however, enough to block the tunnel for some distance. And the water that had turned that clay into mud had come not from the English Channel, nor from any subterranean lake hidden deep below the Channel bed, but from the sprinklers which were carefully designed to deliver several thousand litres of water every minute.

So the tunnel behind compartment 22, which slowly descended to a depth of forty-five metres below the depth of the tunnel at the point where compartment 22 was lying, and which then ascended again to the same level nearer to the tunnel entrance, was blocked with several thousand tons of mud. So far that particular blockage had claimed no victims.

Meanwhile all that the passengers in compartment 22 knew was that they were trapped in the dark, under the English Channel and that with them was the body of a man which had been partially decapitated by a flying disc of ragged plastic. It was, for them, quite enough.

* * *

Slowly Tambroni had investigated the extent of the damage to his wrist. The artery, by some bizarre miracle, had remained undamaged but it was about the only major structure to have escaped. Tendons, muscles and veins had all been torn apart by the flying plastic disc. Without being able to see it Tambroni knew that he'd probably never use that hand again. He'd certainly never play squash again. He tied it tightly with the sleeve torn from his shirt.

Oddly enough it didn't bother him. It really didn't seem to matter at all. It was almost a relief; an excuse to escape from the interminable squash circuit for ever. Never again to have to play against over-confident amateurs, never again to find himself socialising with obese executives and their pathetic, status-conscious wives.

* * *

Miss Millington was thinking of a September day half a century ago. She and her fiancé had been at Weston-super-Mare for the day. They'd gone there on the train with thirty-five others from the local church dramatic group, and it had been the first time that the two of them had the opportunity to be alone for more than a few hurried minutes behind the stage.

Before they caught the train back, Ruby's fiancé had bought her a cheap metal ring with a glass 'sapphire' in its tin setting. He'd put the ring on the third finger of her left hand with all the solemnity of a Bishop performing a marriage ceremony. It was, he explained, only a temporary measure. As soon as he had saved up there would be a real ring, made of real gold and with a real sapphire. Ruby didn't much mind about that. She couldn't have been any happier. And it was after he'd bought her the ring that he'd kissed her. Ruby could still feel his lips pressed on hers with all the innocent urgency of youth. They'd held each other tightly in a bus shelter on the front, and had had to run all the way back to the railway station. The others had teased them and wanted to know where they'd been. Ruby hadn't dared wear the ring when anyone was looking, and when she got home she didn't tell her mother.

In reality there never had been a real ring. There never had been a wedding. And that kiss and cuddle in the bus shelter was all Ruby had to remember of her fiancé. Except for the glass sapphire, of course. She still had that. In the darkness Ruby quietly opened her handbag and reached into the small frayed silk pocket in the lining. Her fingers found the ring straight away and the third finger of her left hand slipped into it easily, as it had done a thousand times before. This time, however, Ruby left the ring in place and firmly shut her handbag. The click startled her and she looked around as if to see if anyone had heard and was staring at her. With her ring on her left hand she could feel her cheeks blushing.

Ruby, at least, was ready for whatever might come.

* * *

Moving Dr Singh's body out of the compartment was more difficult than anyone had foreseen. The hole that he and Benito Tambroni had made was far too small to allow a body through, and Alan Cannon chipped away at the edges of the hole for forty minutes before making it large enough for them to try again.

'How long have we got before the rigor mortis sets in?' asked Cannon.

'In this heat I have no idea,' said Dr Chatwyn.

'He seems stiff already,' said Cannon, struggling to cope with Dr Singh's seemingly infinite number of arms.

'This is crazy,' said Peter Cater suddenly, abandoning his attempt to push Dr Singh's feet through the hole they'd made.

'Why don't we get out of the carriage and leave him behind? If we get out we can perhaps escape.'

Just then Dr Chatwyn's torch expired for the last time. He'd been keeping it trained on the hole while Tambroni and Cannon tried to push Dr Singh's body through. Slowly the light, which had been gently, almost imperceptibly, fading, gave out. They were in blackness again.

'What about the matches?' shouted Cannon. 'Get the matches.'

'There are forty-seven,' said Miss Millington who had faithfully counted their stock of matches when the group had pooled their resources earlier.

'How long can we get light for with forty-seven matches?' asked Tambroni.

'About fifteen or twenty seconds a match,' said Alan Cannon. 'At a guess I'd say about ten minutes.'

'We could make torches,' said Miss Millington.

'Torches?' said someone.

'Alcohol burns,' said Miss Millington. 'We could make old-fashioned sort of torches with bits of cloth and sticks. Dowse them in alcohol and set fire to them.'

'I've got some magazines,' said Peter Cater. 'We could make torches out of those. Just roll them up.'

'They won't burn,' said Alan Cannon. 'Magazines never burn. I've tried burning them when making bonfires in the garden.'

'Rip out the pages and then twist them together tightly,' said Cater. 'They'll burn then.'

'We ought to wait until one of us has got outside before we try that,' Said Dr Chatwyn. 'If we start burning up our oxygen in here we might be in trouble. We need to know how much air there is outside.'

'That's no problem,' said Tambroni. He pushed his head through the hole they'd made, wriggled his shoulders through and then took hold of the outside of the compartment with his left hand. Then he pulled himself through, falling backwards to the ground outside. Since the compartment was angled against the tunnel wall he had only a couple of feet to fall. He bit his lip as he banged his right wrist.

'See how far you can walk,' said Cannon.

'Don't go too far,' shouted James Gower.

'Take some matches,' said Miss Millington. She passed one of the boxes of matches out to Tambroni who took the box gratefully, removed a match, lit it slowly and carefully, and handed back the box for Miss Millington to hold. When he held up the match he could see that for several feet in each direction the tunnel was clear. He turned back to the hole and called through: 'Pass me a couple of those magazines.' The twist of paper that he lit with the second match burnt with a thick black smoke but it provided light for long enough for Alan Cannon and Dr Chatwyn to clamber out of the compartment.

Inside, at the front of the compartment, Mr Black was beginning to sweat. The pain which had started in the centre of his chest had spread to his jaw and was beginning to spread down his left arm. He could feel his fingers tingling.

Peter Cater was next out of the compartment. He helped Miss Millington through. Miss Millington lit another match and set fire to a twist of screwed up magazine pages to give them light. Then came Susan Roberts, Hélène Albric, and Louise and James Black and Gaston Raenackers. James Gower was following, half in and half out of the compartment. Inside there remained only Mr and Mrs Black. Mrs Black realised that something was wrong with her husband only when she heard him gasping for breath. She turned and felt for his arm, only to find him clutching his chest with both hands. She bent forward and in the light from the burning magazines saw the beads of sweat on his forehead.

'David?' she whispered.

'Go on,' said Mr Black with obvious difficulty.

'What is it?'

'Just a pain.'

'Where?'

Mr Black said nothing.

'Can you move?'

'No,' croaked her husband.

'My husband's ill,' shouted Mrs Black in a panic. 'Doctor, please come, doctor!' she called as James Gower climbed, slowly and reluctantly, out through the hole. When Gower had finally managed to extricate himself from the ragged plastic around the edges of the hole, Dr Chatwyn began to climb back through. He went to satisfy Mrs Black and because he felt he ought to go, rather than because he expected to be able to do anything useful. He'd never even seen anyone have a heart attack and he had no idea what to do. Nor did he have a single item of equipment with him. The free sample tablets of Angipax lay forgotten in his briefcase.

As it happened, Dr Chatwyn would probably have been able to do nothing useful if he'd been equipped with oxygen, defibrillator and the usual armamentarium of drugs. By the time Dr Chatwyn got to him, Mr Black was dead, and there were two lifeless bodies in compartment 22.

0340 hrs. August 6th, Sangatte, France

Bleriot's crew had returned from the tunnel. They had gone into the relatively open France-bound tunnel to try to find a way through to the other, blocked tunnel. The deputy engineer had himself met them as they had emerged from the murky distance in their tiny hovercraft. The foreman of the crew was the same man who had led the repair crew into the tunnel a few hours previously to repair the faulty electrical system. He was accompanied by the same two crew members; their football match completely forgotten.

'We can get through,' said the foreman, clambering out of the craft as the younger of his two crew members turned off the power. He was covered from head to toe in thick, dark mud and he walked with considerable difficulty. He'd been lying in the hovercraft with only a few centimetres between his back and the tunnel roof for over an hour.

Bleriot reached out and grasped him by the shoulders, ignoring the mud. 'Are you sure?'

The foreman nodded.

Bleriot turned and ran towards the small group of men standing a few metres away, just out of the muddy pools which stretched out of the tunnel entrance. Garin, who was among them, saw the look of excitement on his face and began to move towards him.

'We've pinpointed it,' said Bleriot. He explained to Garin what the crew had discovered.

'Let's go then,' said Garin. Less than five minutes later they were driving speedily into the France-bound tunnel. It took them just eleven minutes to reach connecting tunnel 49, at the entrance to which one of Raspail's assistants was waiting.

The connecting tunnel, ten metres long and two metres in diameter was designed to allow maintenance crews to move freely into and out of the pilot tunnel. The base was just wide enough to allow one man at a time to walk along it, and Raspail, Bleriot and Garin followed the assistant as he led the way towards the pilot tunnel. The connecting tunnel ended on a small catwalk which ran the entire length of the pilot tunnel. On the other side of the pilot tunnel there was another catwalk. The pilot tunnel itself had a single rail down the centre upon which there usually ran a works engine, a small vehicle which carried the crews and their repair equipment. Steps led down from each connecting tunnel into the pilot tunnel and on the other side steps led up to the opposite connecting tunnel. It was of course possible for repair crews to enter either main tunnel from the pilot tunnel.

That, at least, was the purpose of the pilot tunnel under normal circumstances. It had, however, suffered badly in the explosion. Garin and his colleagues found themselves facing a massive blockage of rock. Their torches picked out an apparently solid wall completely separating them from the connecting tunnel on the other side of the pilot tunnel.

'I thought you said the pilot tunnel was clear here?' said Garin, turning around angrily to face Bleriot.

'It's clearer,' said Bleriot defensively. 'We think we can find a way through here. Further back the pilot tunnel is completely blocked with mud. There's just no way through at all.'

'Where's the train?' asked Raspail.

'About a thousand metres in that direction,' said Bleriot, pointing to the right, diagonally across the pilot tunnel and back towards France.

'Let's get on then,' said Garin. It seemed an impossible task.

'We've got a man in there already,' said Bleriot. He shone his torch downwards until it caught a bright yellow nylon rope. He followed the rope along until it disappeared into a small gap between three large chunks of rock. 'He's been in there for twenty minutes now.'

0345 hrs. August 6th, The Tunnel Train

It would not have been so bad if Mrs Black had become hysterical. Someone could have slapped her face and quietened her down. But her husband's death had shocked her into immobile silence. She sat by his side, hands clenched, and just looked straight ahead of her. After a tantalising taste of the purpose of her life, Mrs Black's world had suddenly been shattered.

Benito Tambroni and Alan Cannon helped James Black back into the compartment to be with his mother. Louise wouldn't go.

'Come on mum,' pleaded James, with tears in his eyes. 'Come with us.' He was glad that it was dark and he couldn't see her or his father. She didn't respond and he had no idea what to do. He leant forward in the dark and spoke again, this time more urgently. 'Come on, mum,' he begged. 'We can't stay in here. Everyone else has got out.'

Mrs Black said nothing and didn't move.

'She won't answer me,' sobbed James, turning back to the hole in the compartment wall. Outside he could see a small flickering light as Tambroni lit another match. It was the eleventh to go up in flames. 'Can't you get her to come out?' said James to Dr Chatwyn.

'She's in shock,' said Dr Chatwyn blankly. 'There isn't anything I can do.' For the hundredth time in an hour he cursed his own clinical incompetence. He felt certain in his heart that he was going to let these people down. They trusted him, his title gave him their respect, but he knew no more than they did about what to do with a woman in severe shock. 'Come out and leave her.'

'We've left our spare clothes inside,' said Tambroni

unexpectedly and angrily. His hand was beginning to cause him a good deal of pain.

'We don't need them,' said Miss Millington. 'It's still hot out here.'

'We need them to make torches of some kind,' explained Tambroni. 'We've got enough matches to last us a few minutes more but after that we're in darkness unless we can make some kind of torch. Magazine pages don't last long enough.'

'There's whisky under my seat,' said James Gower, who hated the dark more than he disliked giving up his whisky.

'I've got some vodka,' said Tambroni. He put his head and shoulders through the gap and wriggled back into the compartment. Without moving more than a few metres away from the hole, he picked up a bottle of whisky, a bottle of vodka and an armful of clothes. He passed the two bottles out to waiting hands, tossed out the clothes and then wriggled back outside again.

'You need something to use as a handle,' said Alan Cannon. 'You can't just set fire to clothes.'

'I've got a small folding umbrella,' offered James Gower. 'I hope my insurance company pays up for all this,' he added, 'I'll expect you to support my claim.'

'Don't worry,' said Tambroni. 'If we get out of here I'll buy you a new umbrella. Where is it?'

'Next to my seat. In my briefcase.'

Tambroni wriggled back into the compartment for a second time. The briefcase was made of expensive calf and locked with a small combination lock. Tambroni handed it out to Gower.

'If we wrap a few shirts and things around it that should be enough,' said Alan Cannon, taking the umbrella from Gower and stooping down to rummage on the floor for pieces of clothing. He wrapped a shirt round the umbrella tightly and then added a tee shirt and a vest.

'We need something to fasten it with,' he said.

'Here, use this,' said Susan Roberts. She reached behind her and unfastened her brassiere. Then she took the umbrella and its new wrapping from Cannon and tied her bra around it several times tightly. She managed to clip the bra fastener securely together so that it kept the other clothes firmly attached to the umbrella.

'Now a little vodka,' said Cannon, picking up one of the bottles. He unfastened the foil at the top of the bottle, removed the cork and sprinkled drops of liquid on to the home-made torch. When he'd finished, he surreptitiously held the bottle to his lips and took a quick swallow.

'Stand back,' said Cannon. The others moved away from where they thought he was. Tambroni, who had by now clambered back out of the compartment again shuffled cautiously away. In the light of the match they could see the odd-looking bundle they had made. It seemed dangerously loose and unsafe. Cannon held the match to the top of the torch and waited until a small fold of shirt material began to smoulder. The flames were small and slow to spread. But they did at least provide some small steady source of light. Thick black smoke curled up from the umbrella as Cannon held it.

'You haven't put enough alcohol on it,' said Tambroni. 'Where's the vodka?'

'Leave it!' shouted Cannon. 'It'll get going in a minute. Anyway, it'll last longer like this.'

Slowly the light from their home-made torch spread until it enabled them to see each other fairly clearly in the tunnel. They could see that the space in which they were all crouching ran for the full length of the compartment. They were crowded into a triangular space made up of the floor and one wall of the tunnel together with the sloping face of the compartment as it leant against the tunnel wall.

Each one of them was shocked by what they saw. Since they'd been trapped in the compartment all they'd seen had been quick glimpses of each other. Now they had time to observe and notice.

Alan Cannon, Peter Cater and Benito Tambroni were all dressed only in their socks and underpants. Their bodies, Tambroni's muscular and lean, Cannon's portly and hairy, Cater's slim and white, were all heavily speckled with blood. In addition, Tambroni's body was covered with scores of small scratches and grazes obtained on his journeys through the hole in the compartment wall. And his right arm ended in a bloody mass of shirt.

Miss Millington wore a long white slip which covered her from neck to knees. All she'd taken off was her dress and her overcoat. She hoped that it had not been among the pile of clothing that Tambroni had thrown out for burning. Astonishingly she still wore her hat, a pale pink little thing with a small crêpe rosette on the front of it. Louise and James Black were holding hands. Louise was dressed in a bikini pants and bra and her brother wore only his boxer shorts. James Gower had taken off only his jacket. He still wore pinstripe trousers and a waistcoat and there were great dark, damp stains of sweat all over both garments. Hélène Albric had taken off her jumper and skirt and her tights. She wore only black silk panties. James Gower liked her to dress without a bra and since they'd met she'd hardly ever worn one. She had already decided that if and when they escaped from the mess they were in she would never again go bra-less.

Dr Chatwyn, wearing just his underpants, was naked to the waist (it was his shirt and vest that were burning). Raenackers had on a string vest. Susan Roberts had always meant to tell him about it but she'd never got around to it. It looked so stupid under those diaphanous nylon shirts he always wore. She, like Hélène Albric, was bra-less. Her bra was wrapped around the smouldering umbrella which Alan Cannon was holding and which was providing the light by which they were all able to see each other. While Hélène Albric stood with her arms across her chest in modesty, Susan Roberts made no attempt to hide herself. Instead she gazed steadily and hungrily at Tambroni, who recognised the look.

Inside the compartment Mrs Black had still not moved. She sat quite still in the darkness, with her husband's body a few inches away from her.

0730 hrs. August 6th, Zürich, Switzerland

It was half-past seven the following morning when Dr Jackson remembered that he had authorised the withdrawal of a vial of smallpox virus from the ACR Basle Laboratory and that the vial had been handed to Dr Singh by Ernest Taylor in Paris. It took him less than fifteen minutes to contact the Channel Tunnel Company in Paris and discover through the emergency telephone number, provided to give relatives and friends information about the disaster, that Dr Singh had been a passenger on the doomed tunnel train.

He sat thoughtfully for a moment before ringing for his personal secretary.

Before lunch, all supplies of smallpox virus in the Basle Laboratory had been destroyed and the laboratory's records had been adjusted accordingly. If anyone ever investigated they would find that Dr Singh could not have obtained smallpox virus from ACR Drogues et Cie for the simple reason that the firm had never possessed any of the virus.

0745 hrs. August 6th, The Tunnel Train

James Gower was thinking of his wife. He knew that his relationship with Hélène would never survive their experience in the tunnel, and somehow it did not seem to matter. For the first time in his life he had learnt to appreciate his wife's virtues; the support and comfort she gave him and the strength which he so badly needed.

He realised for the first time in his life that he needed her. He decided that if he survived he would never again be unfaithful to her; but that he would do his best to make up for the faithless years. At last he appreciated her loyalty and friendship, realising that she had married him for love. It was comforting and warming to know that he was loved. He needed the support of the thought to keep him alive.

When he got back to England he would tell her everything. He'd confess and ask for forgiveness, promising to be faithful and loyal in the future. He knew she would forgive him and he knew she would stay with him. He'd go home every evening and perhaps they would be able to enjoy life together again. He'd take her away for a few weeks; to Venice perhaps. Or to Vienna. Or Berlin. She liked Berlin.

He did not know that his wife was lying only metres away, in a nearby compartment. She had died instantly and never known her husband's good intentions.

* * *

Susan Roberts was changing the dressing on Benito Tambroni's wrist with a tenderness she'd never previously expressed. Ironically, she was using the circular plastic disc which had caused the injury as a splint; using it to keep the half-severed hand in position and to protect the artery from damage.

0800 hrs. August 6th, Rescue Team, The Channel Tunnel

Michel Mortier had been a potholer for seven years. That was why he volunteered when he'd heard about the rocky blockage in the pilot tunnel. He'd volunteered to help check out the connecting tunnels; to see which ones were blocked and which ones were open. Mortier had turned up for his voluntary duties wearing his usual potholing regalia. He had on his rubber waterproof suit, his metal helmet and the battered but powerful mercury cell lamp which clipped on to the front of it. He also carried several hundred feet of thin but strong yellow nylon rope. He'd been into enough potholes to know that you never moved an inch without leaving a trail both for others to follow and for you yourself to use when retreating, if the route became too difficult. Too many potholers had died, lost in the underground warrens they loved to explore.

For the first few metres it was an easy journey. From the comfort of the connecting tunnel and the pilot tunnel catwalk there was one obvious hole to be explored. It was simply a gap formed between three huge lumps of rock. Quite without fear when it came to underground exploring, Mortier had simply scrambled into the hole head-first. His lamp lit up the route and showed him a fairly easy pathway stretching several metres ahead.

After that things had been a little more difficult for half an hour or so. Several times he'd almost been tempted to turn back and once he'd thought he was stuck. Being stuck was something all potholers feared. Mortier could remember reading about an English potholer who'd died of exposure and starvation while stuck underground in a narrow chimney.

Three times he'd arrived at the opposite wall of the pilot tunnel only to discover that the rocks which had fallen in had completely crushed the catwalk and that there was no connecting tunnel in sight. At the fourth attempt, however, Mortier had his first real stroke of luck. He emerged from a gap between two crumbling boulders to find himself directly opposite connecting passageway number 47. And the catwalk outside the passageway was intact. Mortier levered himself up on to it and, stooping low, ran forwards to the next connecting tunnel. The numbers in white paint above the opening told him that he was now at connecting passageway number 46. According to the briefing they'd had, the train was trapped just about fifteen metres away from him.

With his heart beating loudly, partly from exertion and partly from excitement, Mortier moved forwards into the connecting tunnel. There were a few small stones on the floor of the tunnel but there was no mud at all. As he moved forwards he had to step over slightly larger stones, then there were a few pieces of metal and plastic. Finally he was out of the connecting tunnel and on the catwalk in the England-bound tunnel.

Mortier could not believe what he saw. There were pieces of motor car, strips of plastic, lumps of charred rubber and paper all jumbled together in some huge, hideous pot pourri. Mortier had entered the tunnel just at the point where the last of the carriages containing vehicles had been. Somewhere among the tangled wreckage lay the remains of the Blacks' caravan and Mrs Black's washing. Michel Mortier looked around at the devastation and felt filled with despair. He did not believe that anyone could have survived.

0840 hrs. August 6th, The Tunnel Train

While Michel Mortier stared with disbelief and sick horror at the carnage around him, at the wreckage of several million pounds' worth of highly sophisticated machinery and safety equipment, the passengers in compartment 22 were standing still and quiet while Alan Cannon moved along with his home-made torch. The flickering light illuminated the outside of the still intact compartment which had been damaged only very slightly in the explosion.

At its front end, where the coupling should have attached it to the penultimate compartment, Cannon shone his light on to an impenetrable wall of rock. Several pieces of metal and plastic glinted in the light. Although they did not know it, compartment 22 had broken away from the rest of the train and skidded off the rails alone. The nearest compartment, now the last one of the passenger train, was thirty or forty metres away. And in front of compartment 22 the ceiling of the tunnel had collapsed entirely, allowing several thousand tons of rock and rubble to fall into the tunnel, together with the huge mild-steel facing plates and the concrete segments which had made up the roof itself. By some miracle, compartment 22 was relatively unscathed. The tunnel roof had held firm. The left-hand side of the compartment, now effectively the top, was covered with small pieces of rock and smashed and shattered pieces from the train. The only space unfilled was that small triangle of space hidden underneath the train, in the angle it made with the right hand tunnel wall.

At the other end of compartment 22, Cannon's torch picked out no rocks, no debris and no fractured artefacts. Instead there was just clay. The clay had crept into the small space in which most of the remaining twelve passengers were crowded. It was thick, wet, blueish and crumbly.

'If we're going to try and get out of here we ought to be going that way,' said Tambroni, pointing towards the clay.

'Why?' demanded Gower, defiantly.

'At least we can dig through the clay,' said Tambroni, 'We can't possibly get through rock with our bare hands.'

It made sense. Gower said nothing more.

0915 hrs. August 6th, Zürich, Switzerland

Bruckner, Jackson and Meier had already been at work for an hour and a half. The Swiss always believe in getting to work early. It's one of the things that gives them a head start over the rest of Europe.

'But we don't know that the explosion had anything to do with our chemicals,' insisted Meier for the tenth time in as many minutes. 'I admit that these chemicals can be dangerous but we've never had any problem with them.'

'I don't think for a moment that they spontaneously ignited,' said Dr Jackson, his patience running out. 'But they could easily have made an explosion worse. It was because of the risk of adding to the fire hazard that the Channel Tunnel Company originally banned all potentially explosive materials.'

'I think Dr Jackson is right,' said Bruckner. He hadn't spoken for several minutes and the other two had almost forgotten that he was there. When he spoke, however, they listened carefully. 'We must assume that there is a certain amount of potential trouble in this for us, and act accordingly.'

'So what do we do?' asked Dr Jackson.

'We sue them,' smiled Bruckner.

The other two just stared at him.

'We get our lawyers to sue the Channel Tunnel Company,' explained Bruckner. 'We demand compensation for the materials we've lost. And we add another lawsuit for loss of earnings.'

'I don't see...,' began Meier.

'The Channel Tunnel Company carries insurance covering structural faults,' explained Bruckner. 'But their policy does not cover a cargo explosion.'

Slowly, Meier began to understand.

'If we threaten them with a lawsuit,' Bruckner went on, 'I think you'll find that the Channel Tunnel Company will suddenly be able to prove to the world that their collapse was an accident, caused by a structural weakness. No one will bother studying the cargo.' He pushed back his chair and looked at his watch. 'I really must be moving,' he apologised.

1130 hrs. August 6th, The Tunnel Train

Despite the fact that the home-made torch was giving off a moderate amount of light, and the hole in the compartment wall was now about a metre across, it was still quite dark inside compartment 22. Dark enough for those scrabbling around inside for items of clothing and other personal bits and pieces to be able to pretend that neither Dr Singh nor Mr Black were in there with them. And dark enough for them to avoid looking at Mrs Black who was still sitting motionless and silent by her husband's side.

Very slowly a tear was forming in the corner of Mrs Black's left eye and, almost imperceptibly, it began to creep down the crease between her nose and left cheek. As it fell away it gathered speed until it was caught in the tiny blonde hairs on her upper lip. A second tear formed a moment or two later and followed the same route. And then a third, this time travelling from the right eye. Soon tears were falling in a steady stream, dropping from Mrs Black's cheeks and chin and landing silently on her lap.

Mrs Black did not return to consciousness suddenly; she drifted back slowly and step by step. And as she returned, as she remembered where she was and what had happened, as she became fully aware that her husband was dead, as she became conscious of the fact that her children were no longer with her, she began to scream.

It was not a single scream. As the echoes of the first scream died down, Mrs Black took a deep involuntary breath and started to scream again. And again, and again.

'See if you can help her,' said Susan Roberts to Hélène Albric. She recognised a tenderness in the other woman; knew instinctively that Hélène could offer more comfort. 'Take Louise with you,' she added in a whisper.

Obediently, unquestioningly, Hélène stood up and walked across to where she could see Louise. Then the two of them climbed into the compartment and moved to the front row where Louise's mother was sitting. They sat on her left, with Louise in between Hélène and her mother, gaining comfort from the one to pass on to the other. She stroked her mother's arm, held her face with the other hand, and whispered gently to her. In that moment, Louise Black grew into a young woman, abandoning for ever the innocence and naiveté of childhood.

Slowly, Mrs Black's screams turned to sobs. She began to cry compulsively and unceasingly, her body heaving and shaking uncontrollably. While Louise and Hélène comforted her, the others slowly returned to what they were doing. And Gaston Raenackers simply sank deeper and deeper into his corner of the train, the corner furthest from Mrs Black, and began to rock himself gently, backwards and forwards, backwards and forwards.

1200 hrs. August 6th, Rescue Team, The Channel Tunnel

Following the rope he'd trailed behind him, Mortier found his way back to the tunnel where he'd left Garin, Bleriot and Raspail. His expression told them everything they feared.

'So what do we do?' asked Raspail, when Mortier had reported.

'Can we drill straight through from here to the place where the train is?' Garin asked him.

'We'll have to use a lightweight pneumatic rock drill. There isn't room to operate a large drill, even if we could get one here in time to do anything useful.'

'How long to get through?' asked Garin.

'It's between twenty-five and thirty metres, said Raspail thoughtfully. 'I doubt if anyone has ever tackled anything like this before.'

'We can bring a truck into the main tunnel to France,' said Garin.

'Ten, twelve hours,' suggested Raspail. 'Maybe more, maybe less. It depends on how much luck we have.'

'Get going then,' said Garin. He looked at his watch, 'Can you get two teams working? Drill two passage tunnels through into the England-bound tunnel.'

'I suppose so,' said Raspail. 'I'll have to bring equipment from the nearest tunnelling site.'

'Where's that?'

'There's a tunnel under construction in Norway,' said Raspail. 'The site engineer is an old friend of mine. I can get the stuff here within an hour, maybe two. I'll need a large helicopter. Preferably two.'

'Get whatever you need,' said Garin. 'Don't haggle over costs. Just get it fast.'

1235 hrs. August 6th, The Tunnel Train

Tambroni and Cannon had decided that if they dug a tunnel leading upwards through the wall of clay, they would not only stand a chance of getting through the clay, but would also, if they were lucky, find themselves on top of the blockage. There was a chance, they agreed, that the clay did not reach up to the tunnel roof. As added support for their theory, Cannon had pointed out that if they tunnelled along through the bottom part of the clay there would be a good chance of having a roof-fall; whereas if they tunnelled along in the top part of the clay there would be no chance of that.

They decided to dig their tunnel at an angle of approximately forty-five degrees since that gave them a good chance to avoid a roof-fall, and did not make it too difficult for them to work.

The only spade-like implements they had were Tambroni's squash rackets. With a sigh of regret, Tambroni began the excavation, plunging his racket deep into the clay wall with his weakened left hand firmly gripping the handle. He pulled down, then up, on the handle, levering at the clay. All that happened was that the racket bent at the point where the twin-stalked handle joined the frame. The racket head remained half buried in the clay. It was clearly going to be even more difficult than they had imagined.

'Try chipping out small pieces,' suggested Peter Cater, who was holding the torch.

Reaching behind him for the second racket, Tambroni nodded. He pushed the racket head a couple of inches into the clay so that it cut out a small triangular wedge of the heavy blue-grey material. With a few extra jabs of the racket they managed to remove the wedge. They had made the first few inches of their tunnel.

'We need something to help carry the clay away," said Cannon, picking up the almost solid piece of clay and fingering at it. 'We'll soon be up to our knees in the stuff.'

'There are some plastic shopping bags in the compartment,' suggested Peter Cater.

'Or my sports bag,' said Tambroni.

Cannon shook his head and handed the lump of clay to Tambroni.

'Feel that. It's too heavy for any bag we've got.'

'We need a wheelbarrow,' said Tambroni with a grin.

'Wait a minute!' said Cater; he handed the torch to Cannon and scurried back towards the hole into the compartment. He leapt through and a moment or two later called to them both.

'Come and give me a hand,' he called. From the sounds he was making it was clear that he was kicking and heaving at something.

Tambroni and Cannon started for the compartment entrance together. Dr Chatwyn and Susan Roberts met them there.

If we can get one of these seats out,' said Cater, appearing back at the home-made doorway, 'we can dump the clay on it and drag it along.'

Tambroni and Cannon looked at each other. Cannon nodded first, then Tambroni smiled.

'Great idea!' said Cannon to Cater. 'But can we get it out?'

'It's only held on by a few screws,' said Cater. 'And if we bust those off there are two steel runners forming the base. It'll slide quite easily.'

They had the seat wrenched away from its mounting within a couple of minutes. Tipped on to its back runner, with one person pushing on the back of the seat and another pulling on the front, it made a crude but effective wheelbarrow.

'Clear the floor,' ordered Tambroni. 'We need as smooth a surface as we can get. We'll dump the clay at the far end there. Pack it as tightly as you can.'

'Benito and I will dig,' said Cannon. He pointed to Peter Cater and Dr Chatwyn. 'You move the wheelbarrow.'

'I'll stack the clay,' said Susan Roberts. 'We need to keep it tightly packed or we'll run out of room.'

'I don't know who you people think you are, taking charge like this,' said James Gower, suddenly and unexpectedly. 'No one has appointed you as leaders.'

'No, they haven't,' said Susan Roberts. 'But this plan is the only one we have at the moment and your contributions to date have been precisely nil. I suggest you damned well help. Someone's got to make sure the floor is kept clear of bits of clay or else moving the barrow is going to be impossible.'

'I will certainly do no such thing,' said Gower, indignantly. Despite the incredible heat he still wore his waistcoat. His shirt, such of it as could be seen, was soaked with sweat.

'Yes you will,' said Tambroni coldly.

Gower began to say something but clearly thought better of it. Even with one arm totally disabled and the other arm severely weakened, Tambroni did not look like a man to argue with.

'Let's get on with it then,' said Cannon. 'We've got a lot of digging to do.'

Inside the compartment, Hélène Albric and Louise Black still sat and comforted Mrs Black. Miss Millington and James Black were sorting out the miscellaneous collection of clothes. Gaston Raenackers, forgotten by all, sat at the back of the compartment his eyes closed and his hands clenched tightly around his knees. Just as Mrs Black had returned to reality so he had left it.

* * *

His arms aching, his shoulders weary and his fingers numb, Cannon stopped digging for a moment. He wondered if the police had found the woman in Montmartre and for the tenth time in as many minutes found himself trying to remember exactly what she had looked like. Would the police, he wondered, just accept her death as natural and forget all about it? Or would they have started a hunt for her killer? Would there be anyone who had seen him going into her room? Had anyone seen him leave? Was there anything there to lead them to him? If they had found his fingerprints there, could they trace him? He tried to remember whether or not he'd ever had his fingerprints taken. There had been a time when everyone in the neighbourhood over the age of 16 had been finger-printed by the police who had been looking for a man who had raped a student at a college near to his home. Cannon wondered if they'd have kept all the fingerprints. He seemed to remember that they'd promised to destroy the prints they'd taken but would they have done that? Somehow he doubted it.

While he was trapped in the tunnel they might have already identified him. They would have traced him to his hotel where staff would have confirmed that the man they were looking for seemed worried and anxious. They'd have checked with the airport and then the railway station and discovered that he'd caught the train to Sangatte. Once they'd done that, it would not have taken them long to discover that he was trapped inside the tunnel. Or killed. They wouldn't know whether he was still alive or not. Perhaps he could convince them that he was someone else. Perhaps he could emerge from the crash with a new name and a new personality. None of the other passengers knew his real identity. He could claim that his papers had all been destroyed. He could make sure that they were. That at least would give him some breathing space; some time to get away from the police.

He wondered whether they'd emerge on the English side of the channel or on the French side. Somehow he didn't doubt that they would emerge. Being trapped in the tunnel was a real, soluble problem. It was the police he was really frightened of. That was something over which he had absolutely no control.

At least there wouldn't be any friends or relatives to meet him and give the game away. Of that he was fairly sure. There wasn't anyone to care, and no one knew exactly where he was or how he was getting back from Paris. They didn't even know he had been to Paris.

That was it, he decided, he'd find a new name. He would emerge from the tunnel as someone else and Alan Cannon would be lost forever.

Calmed again for a moment, Cannon carried on chipping and scraping his way through the wall of mud.

* * *

In crises different people are kept alive by different driving forces. James Black was inspired by anger and by bitterness; anger at the person or persons whose incompetence had led to the death of his father, and bitterness because of his own bereavement.

James and his father had had little in common, it is true, but for the first time in his life James had found a specific, identifiable target for the rage which had been burning inside him for years. And in death his father had acquired qualities and inspired memories he would never have merited in life. James Black was secretly but firmly committed to avenging his father's death.

That commitment would, of course, disappear entirely when he was rescued and the need for survival had passed. Then James would once again become a frightened, unhappy, poorly balanced boy.

* * *

The small metal box that Dr Singh had carried in his pocket lay opened on the floor of the compartment. The tiny vial which contained the deadly smallpox virus had fallen out of the box and lay unprotected for several hours before Susan Roberts trod on it and broke it. She was in the compartment hunting for a bottle of water. The heat, and their exertions, meant that they were all sweating heavily.

'What's the matter?' asked Tambroni, hearing her yelp.

'I've trodden on some glass,' said Susan. 'I don't know what it was but I don't think its too bad.'

'Are you bleeding?'

'Not much,' said Susan. 'Nothing to worry about.' She bent down and brushed the broken pieces of glass underneath the nearest seat so that no one else would tread on them.

* * *

To his own surprise, Benito Tambroni did not feel particularly dismayed at facing the future with only one useful hand. There was no doubt in his mind that he would never again be able to wield a squash racket. But somehow it didn't matter in the slightest. The accident had suddenly and unexpectedly provided him with an excuse to abandon his fading career as a professional sportsman. An excuse which promised him the peace and contentment which he might otherwise have never found.

He had no idea what he would do if they managed to escape from the tunnel. But it didn't really matter very much. Whatever it was, he would be much more likely to find satisfaction and happiness than he had been able to while running as fast as he could to stand still in the world of competitive squash. Of that, at least, he was certain. And that certainly gave him strength to continue to fight for himself and the others who, he knew, were relying on him.

* * *

It was while she was scavenging in the compartment, looking for things to burn, that Miss Millington found the first of Peter Cater's Roman coins. She found the second a few moments later. Carefully and casually she put the two coins into her purse. She didn't recognise the coins and certainly had no idea of their value; but she correctly assumed that they were suitable enough in weight and size to be used in a telephone coin box or public lavatory.

1500 hrs. August 6th, Leicester Square, London

From Heathrow Airport, Dr Thaier, the European Credit Bank's replacement representative, was driven straight to the ACR Offices in Leicester Square. Once there, it took less than twenty minutes for the papers involving the exchange of the Willenhall factory to be completed and signed.

At 1530, with Dr Thaier comfortably installed in the guest stateroom on the fifth floor of the ACR building, George Yallop, who, as well as being the Managing Director of Prophax Pharmaceuticals, was the senior London representative of the ACR holding company, was on the telephone to Dr Bruckner in Zürich, using a scrambled line kept permanently available between the two cities.

When he confirmed with the firm's financial director that the control of the property had changed hands successfully, Yallop spoke to Dr Jackson and Willey Meier, who together confirmed that replacement consignments of the chemicals necessary for the production of Angipax were on their way to England.

'The tunnel looks like being out of commission for some time,' said Dr Jackson resignedly. 'We will keep you supplied with as much of the two chemicals as you need. It's not as quick but we'll ship the stuff over by sea in container lorries.'

1515 hrs. August 6th, Sangatte, France

Thomas Raspail had not gone home. He had telephoned his wife from the control room but he'd warned her that he did not know when he would be back. Then he'd paced around the control room like some caged animal desperately searching for freedom. Thomas Raspail considered himself morally responsible for the safety of all passengers travelling through the tunnel, and could no more go home and sleep than he could drive past a road accident. He had never been one of those people who worry about legal responsibilities, insurance companies and limited liabilities. Raspail knew himself what his liabilities and responsibilities were.

Eventually, he had headed back into the France-bound tunnel that he'd left less than an hour previously. He ordered the driver of the small rescue vehicle that had carried Garin, Bleriot and himself into the tunnel a little while before, to take him back to connecting tunnel 47. The driver thought nothing of this; it seemed to him quite a natural order; he assumed that Raspail was merely going back to check on some aspect of the rescue.

When he arrived at connecting tunnel 47 Raspail thanked the driver, told him that he'd be some time and suggested that he return to the tunnel entrance. The driver, who never felt entirely comfortable underneath the English Channel, happily agreed.

Raspail then returned back to the junction of connecting tunnel 47 with the pilot tunnel. He'd brought with him a rubber-covered torch and he wriggled into the gap through which had seen Mortier disappear. If anyone had seen him and asked what he was doing, Raspail would have had to admit that he had no idea what he hoped to achieve; he had no plan and certainly no intention of becoming a hero. He simply could not sit around and wait for the drilling crew to get through to the trapped train.

1530 hrs. August 6th, The Tunnel Train

In the first hour and a half they managed to dig a tunnel about two metres long. They had had to sacrifice one of Tambroni's squash rackets to make another torch. They had wrapped clothes around the handle, using Miss Millington's brassiere to keep the collection of materials wrapped tightly together. The other two rackets they used together as trowels, although they found themselves using their hands just as much as the rackets. It was easier to dig away at the clay with outstretched fingers than with the rounded racket heads.

While Tambroni and Cannon dug away at the top of the tunnel, taking it in turns to work on the face or to help pull the lumps of clay down the tunnel to where Peter Cater and Dr Chatwyn were waiting to load up the wheelbarrow, Susan Roberts kept the discarded clay packed tightly against the far wall where it rested against the rocky fall. Miss Millington still busied herself preparing strips of material with which they could prepare fresh torches. They had only nine matches left and they were trying to ensure that each fresh torch could be lit from a dying torch. Moaning and reluctant, James Gower kept the floor clear of clay, kicking at the pieces which fell from the wheelbarrow and pushing them underneath the carriage.

The heat was becoming more intense by the minute and the shortage of oxygen was making every movement difficult, even painful.

'How high do you think this tunnel is?' asked Peter Cater, as he and Dr Chatwyn pulled and pushed their makeshift wheelbarrow with its load of clay to where Susan Roberts waited, her breasts glistening with sweat and smeared with clay.

'Six or seven metres,' guessed Chatwyn. 'Judging by what I can remember of the entrance to the tunnel.'

'How long till they reach the top?' asked Cater.

Chatwyn cursed as he stumbled on a lump of clay that Gower had not moved.

'They've done a couple of metres in an hour,' said Cater hopefully.

'They'll slow down as they get higher,' Chatwyn pointed out. 'It'll get more and more difficult and they'll get tired.'

'How far do you think they've got to dig?'

'At the angle they're taking it'll be about ten metres up to the roof,' said Chatwyn. 'Six hours if we're lucky.'

Cater wished he hadn't asked.

* * *

Dr Chatwyn's estimate proved to be unexpectedly pessimistic. It took only three hours for them to reach the tunnel roof. Alan Cannon and Tambroni worked throughout to dig a way through they clay. They had eventually abandoned the rackets altogether and chosen to use their hands. To their relief, the clay became lighter and easier to move the higher they climbed. After an hour and a half they found that they could dig out great chunks of clay with one hand. So quickly were they moving that Cannon actually bruised his hand on a piece of the tunnel ceiling when they finally reached the top of their climb. The pain, however, was immediately forgotten in the joy he felt. He turned round, knocking a small avalanche of clay into Tambroni's upturned face.

'We're at the top!' he called. He reached up to bang on the tunnel roof and lost his footing in the small steps they'd dug for themselves. Scrabbling desperately to try and get a footing he and Tambroni slid down their small tunnel, crashing harmlessly into a heap at the bottom where Peter Cater and Dr Chatwyn looked anxiously on.

They celebrated by resting for a while. Then, ten minutes later, Tambroni climbed slowly up the ten-metre tunnel. It was too small for a torch to be carried and he was in complete darkness. Wriggling forwards, using his head as a battering ram and his one good hand as a spade, Tambroni managed to extend the tunnel one metre forwards in less than ten minutes. At the top of the tunnel the clay was softer, lighter and less compressed.

In the next two hours, he and Cannon travelled forwards nearly fifty metres. At ten-metre intervals, they made the tunnel slightly wider, giving themselves small recesses where they could change places, taking the lead in turn.

Cannon was the leader when they made their second breakthrough. The air in their narrow tunnel through the clay was even hotter and staler than the air had been below in the compartment. So the air in the space into which they broke through, although it too was stale and hot, seemed fresh and clean by comparison. For a moment or two Cannon could not understand why he could move his head and shoulders freely from side to side. He had grown so accustomed to moving forwards with his eyes closed that it took him a moment or two to decide to try opening them. Then, when he blinked, he found himself looking at the ceiling and in front of him a surface of clay stretching as far as he could see. It was still dark but for someone who had been buried alive in a veritable mountain of clay it was as light and cheerful a sight as a sunny day in the countryside. He broke out with the rest of his body and revelled in the freedom. He could move his legs sideways as well as forwards and backwards. Behind him Tambroni followed him out of their tunnel. Below them there was still a mass of clay some six metres thick. But they were now lying on top of the clay instead of having to burrow through it.

'You go back and tell the others,' said Cannon to Tambroni. 'I'll go and get help.'

They shook hands and parted. That was the last time that anyone saw Alan Cannon alive.

1655 hrs. August 6th, Zürich, Switzerland

Ernest Taylor never failed to be impressed by the luxury of the main offices of the ACR Drogues Company. Most of his working life was spent "on the road", and although that rather outdated phrase did not fully describe the unending sequence of five-star hotels and first class aeroplane tickets that made up Taylor's business tours, not even the most luxurious hotels outdid the ACR Drogues headquarters.

Taylor was waiting in Dr Jackson's personal ante-room, which was furnished with half a dozen leather arm chairs and a low mahogany table carrying copies of *The New Yorker*, *Economist*, *Time*, *Express*, and half a dozen financial daily papers. There was a pair of Stubbs paintings on the walls. Dr Jackson's personal secretary and two typists occupied a rather larger office, the route to which lay through one of the three doors in the ante-room. Of the other two, one was the outer door, leading to the corridor, and the other led into Dr Jackson's personal suite which consisted of an office, bathroom and bedroom.

Taylor was halfway through a *New Yorker* article on the plight of the modern American Indian when the ACR Drogue medical director's secretary strode briskly out of her office into the anteroom, and smiled at Taylor.

'Dr Jackson will see you now, Mr Taylor.'

Taylor stood, put the *New Yorker* back on to the table and pulled down his jacket. He followed the secretary into Dr Jackson's office.

'It's good to see you again,' said Dr Jackson after a few polite preliminaries. 'But there must be something important for you to come chasing down to Zürich to see me. What is it?' He stretched back in his luxurious black leather swivel chair, and waited.

'Do you remember seeing a Dr Singh a few months ago?' asked Taylor. 'He's a cardiologist who specialises in pharmacology or a pharmacologist who specialises in cardiology. I can never remember which. You met him with me in Geneva.'

Jackson thought for a moment. 'Arrogant, pushy sort of fellow, if I remember right?'

Taylor nodded.

'What's happened? He wrote a paper for us didn't he? Didn't he do some research on Angipax and write it up for one of those specialist journals? I'm damned if I can remember which one.' He waved towards a pile of journals on a table on the far side of his room. Apart from the pile, which must have been three feet high, there were several dozen current issues of other journals neatly arranged on special shelving so that their covers could all be seen. 'If I read all of them I'd never do anything else.'

'I met him in Paris recently and handed over to him a vial of smallpox virus,' said Taylor. 'You must remember that. The authorisation came through you.'

Jackson shook his head. 'I don't remember that.' He frowned. 'We don't hand out smallpox viruses.'

'It was from our laboratory in Basle,' said Taylor.

'Basle?' said Dr Jackson. 'They don't keep smallpox there.'

He thought for a moment. 'In fact,' he went on, 'I'm sure we don't keep smallpox anywhere. It's banned now. We'd have to have special dispensation from the World Health Organisation.'

'He wanted some for a research project,' insisted Taylor. 'He agreed to do that paper for Angipax for us and to let us have the commercial rights to his research.'

'We certainly have options on a lot of research projects,' said Dr Jackson. 'It's a common clause we insist on when we fund a research programme.'

'But the smallpox virus came from your office,' said Taylor.

'Look, Taylor,' said the medical director, standing up. 'You're a good salesman and I like you. But don't tell me what I have and have not done.'

'Singh was on the train that got caught in the tunnel explosion,' said Taylor, who'd also stood up. 'I'm pretty sure he had the smallpox with him.'

'I think you ought to have a couple of weeks' rest, old chap,' said Dr Jackson, coming round his desk and putting a hand on Taylor's arm. 'Why don't you take a holiday? Use the company lodge in the Bahamas. Take your wife with you.'

'I'm divorced, sir,' said Taylor coldly. 'And I had a holiday a month ago.' He turned round and walked quickly out of the room. He understood what was happening and he didn't like it one little bit.

1810 hrs. August 6th, Paris

Philippe Garin was exhausted. He had travelled by helicopter to the Paris heliport and driven to the place Vendôme in a hired car that had been waiting there for him. It was ten minutes past six when he stumbled into the Channel Tunnel Company headquarters.

'They're in the board room,' said the receptionist, a tall redhead with an undisguised affection for Garin. 'They asked me to tell you to go straight in.'

'Thanks,' muttered Garin.

'Can I get you anything?'

Garin shook his head.

'Coffee?'

'Thank you, yes. That would be nice,' smiled Garin. 'Will you send some up?'

In the board room Janine Boysee was the only one who smiled when Garin entered.

'Come in, sit down,' ordered Claude Noiret sharply. 'We're waiting for you.'

'I think M.Garin has been rather busy in Sangatte,' said Mme Boysee.

'I'm sure he has,' agreed Noiret coldly. He waited while Garin sat. 'What is the latest situation?'

Garin explained the situation as best he could, pointing out that the England-bound tunnel was blocked and that it was estimated that a large number of people were trapped in the wreckage.

'Have you any idea what caused the collapse?' asked Sir Frederick.

'None, I'm afraid,' replied Garin.

Noiret raised an eyebrow.

'We've been concentrating on trying to get into the tunnel. We have to assume that there are people alive in there.'

'And have you? Got into the tunnel?'

'Not yet.'

'When are you likely to get in?' asked Morgensdorf.

'I'm afraid it will probably be a few hours yet.'

'Hours? What are your people doing?' asked Noiret.

'Everything they can,' answered Garin quickly. 'They've been working non-stop. Some of them are risking their lives to get into the tunnel.'

'Would you like some coffee, M. Garin?' asked Janine Boysee suddenly and unexpectedly. The receptionist had entered quietly and, unnoticed, had put down a tray of coffee on the small table behind Mme. Boysee.

'Thank you,' said Garin. 'I came straight from the tunnel,' he explained to the others. No one else spoke.

'Have you ruled out sabotage?' asked Mme. Boysee.

Garin shook his head. 'We haven't ruled anything out yet.'

'What do you think happened?' asked Sir Frederick.

'I'm not sure. There was an explosion. That's all we know. I don't think it will help to guess.'

'But is the collapse the sort that could have occurred as a

result of any structural weakness?' asked Sir Frederick.

'I don't think so,' said Garin cautiously.

'I've had a number of enquiries from commercial groups,' said Noiret. 'They're worried about the length of delays likely to affect future shipments.'

'I'm afraid there are bound to be delays,' said Garin.

'Yes,' agreed Noiret. 'But we must have more precise details.'

'I'm afraid I can't give you anything more precise just yet.' Garin found it impossible to hide his disgust.

'The reason for my interest in the possible cause of the collapse is simple to explain,' said Noiret quietly. 'We have already received a large liability claim from a major European drugs manufacturer – ACR Drogues. If the collapse was caused by a structural weakness, then there is a good chance that we will be able to obtain support from our insurers. If it was an Act of God or a result of terrorist action, then we'll get no help,' he smiled. 'For some reason, insurance companies put God and terrorists in the same category.'

'My security officer is convinced that there was no chance of any terrorist activity,' said Garin.

'And you don't feel that the extent of the damage is explained by a simple collapse – an Act of God?

Garin shook his head.

'In addition to the claim from the Swiss pharmaceutical company which has lost a considerable quantity of valuable merchandise on that train there are bound to be personal accident and injury claims,' Sir Frederick pointed out.

'I've got to have something to tell our lawyers,' said Noiret.

Suddenly Garin had had enough. He got up and walked out without saying another word. He stopped his driver twice on the route back to the heliport; once to buy a thermos flask and once to stop at a café, fill up the flask, and buy a bag full of fresh croissants.

1840 hrs. August 6th, Rescue Team, Channel Tunnel

Wearing breathing equipment, ear muffs and dust-tight suit, Bleriot watched carefully as the first of his two drilling crews cleared a temporary obstruction in their vacuum cleaning machine; essential to keep their working area relatively free of dust and small pieces of rock. Without the machine, their working area would soon become waist deep in slivers and particles of rock.

The drilling machinery had arrived in Sangatte within an hour and three-quarters. Within fifteen minutes of its arrival, the crews were setting up the drills and preparing to begin tunnelling through to the train in the other major tunnel.

Inspired by professional pride, a bonus and possibly by side bets, the two crews were racing each other for the honour of making the first breakthrough. The crew that Bleriot was watching were in the lead by half a metre or so. The drilling foreman had confirmed Bleriot's estimate that they would break through into the England-bound tunnel within ten hours. The two experts had confirmed that with some luck, no break downs and an encouraging bonus arrangement, there was an excellent chance that the breakthrough would come in less time.

For Bleriot there was nothing but waiting and wondering where Thomas Raspail had gone. The drilling crews knew their work well enough. Originally, Bleriot had intended to handle the machinery with his own men, but the Norwegian firm which had lent the equipment had offered the services of its own drillers. This was not entirely a charitable gesture; the equipment was worth several million American dollars and could easily be damaged in inexpert hands.

* * *

While Bleriot watched the drilling operation and Garin sat impatiently in his helicopter as it approached Sangatte, Thomas Raspail lay semi-conscious in a small rock gully in the pilot tunnel. He'd entered the rocky maze which filled the pilot tunnel with no safety helmet, no ropes to help guide him in and out and only an ordinary torch to provide illumination. At first he'd moved quickly and comparatively easily, wriggling along through narrow passageways between some of the larger lumps of rock which had fallen in from above. The cuts and scratches he'd received had hardly worried him; he was satisfied to know that he was doing something.

It wasn't until he'd been in the pilot tunnel for the greater part of an hour that he'd realised that he had no idea of what direction he was supposed to be taking. Squirming and turning in the tunnel he'd completely lost all sense of direction. Without a rope to guide him back he had no way of knowing just where he'd come from. And to make matters worse he seemed to have got himself stuck.

He found himself in a small opening between two huge grey rocks and in the dim light of his fading torch had noticed only one possible exit route. To the naked eye it looked no smaller than any of the other passageways he'd gone through. But when it came to it he found himself well and truly fixed. He couldn't pull himself through; nor could he pull himself back. He was stranded with his head, shoulders and upper chest in a narrow gap underneath a flat-bottomed rock and his lower chest, abdomen and legs left in the opening between the two grey rocks. The rock pressing on his chest was making it difficult for him to breathe; he felt as though it was crushing the life out him. His arms were stretched out in front of him and his torch had rolled forwards and out of reach. The feeble beam of light it gave out was wasted on a small circle of featureless rock.

Thomas Raspail was stuck, stranded and lost. It took him four hours to die.

1845 hrs. August 6th, Zürich, Switzerland

For once in his life, Ernest Taylor was determined not to be ignored or dismissed as an idiot. After leaving Dr Jackson's office, he had made his way to the Chairman's suite. Rather to his surprise he'd found himself being ushered into Mr Huber's personal office.

The Chairman listened attentively while Taylor told his story.

'I appreciate you coming to me with this,' he said, with a hand on Taylor's shoulder. 'You're the sort of honest, decent employee this company really needs. We live in a world which is sometimes rather too corrupt and concerned only with profit. Our industry has to work hard to maintain the trust of the public and people like you help us do that.' He paused and looked directly at the salesman for a moment. 'In your shoes I hope that I would have done exactly what you have done.' He sighed, and took his hand off Taylor's shoulder. 'I hope I would have had your courage.'

Taylor looked down at his shoes. He felt embarrassed.

'I'm afraid the problem is that Dr Jackson has not been entirely honest with you,' said Mr Huber. 'The truth is that we don't have any supplies of smallpox virus ourselves. When Dr Singh made this request, Dr Jackson came to me and asked if we had access to any of the World Health Organisation stores of the virus. I told him we didn't and that even if we did I wouldn't sanction such a deal.'

Taylor frowned. He didn't understand.

'The vial that you handed to Dr Singh contained nothing more virulent than chickenpox virus,' lied Huber. 'He shook his head sadly. 'I don't approve of the subterfuge, of course,' he went on. 'But Dr Jackson felt that under the circumstances it was the best course of action he could follow. He believes very strongly that to deny people the opportunity to benefit from Angipax would be medically improper.' He paused and reached out to touch the representative again. 'I must ask you to treat all this as entirely confidential, I hope that in time you will learn to forgive Dr Jackson and myself for this small but well-intentioned deception and regard Dr Jackson and myself with the level of respect which I know he and I have for you.'

Taylor started to protest, but the Chairman would have none of it. Before the remonstration could begin he'd opened the door and smilingly ushered the representative out. As soon as Taylor had gone, the Chairman picked up his telephone and dialled Jackson's number.

Anyone who had heard both the conversation with Taylor and the one with the medical director would have suddenly realised exactly why Huber had become the Chairman of one of the largest and most powerful companies in the world.

Until he'd heard Taylor's story Hubert hadn't even heard of Dr Singh and his smallpox virus. The explanation Huber had offered, and which had been so readily believed and accepted, had been prepared entirely on the spur of the moment.

1850 hrs. August 6th, The Tunnel Train

When Tambroni returned to the compartment, the others received his news with many different responses.

Peter Cater and Dr Chatwyn, who were sitting on the clay-covered chair they'd been using as a wheelbarrow, both had to struggle to keep back the tears of joy they felt bursting to flood down their cheeks. Instead they solemnly shook hands with each other.

Miss Millington unashamedly threw her arms around young James Black and hugged him. She had grown very fond of James and was happier more for his prospect of escape than her own. She had thrown herself into the task of preparing material for the flaming torches which lit up their semi-artificial cavern so eerily, and had enjoyed a sense of pride in having a job to do which had some immediate value. James Black, too proud to allow himself the luxury of tears, had found Miss Millington's company encouraging and supportive.

James Gower, shattered by the loss of dignity and status – which he felt, had disappeared with the eventual loss of his waistcoat, shirt and trousers – was too numb to register any appreciation of Tambroni's news. He stared at Tambroni dumbly for a moment or two, nodded once and turned away to sit down on the floor, alone.

Inside the compartment Mrs Black, Louise and Hélène Albric were still sitting together on the front row. Mrs Black and Louise were both asleep, while Hélène, keeping a watchful eye on them both, was also having considerable difficulty in staying awake.

Gaston Raenackers, still quiet and rocking gently on his seat, showed no apparent sign of having even heard Tambroni's shout of joy.

Susan Roberts greeted Tambroni with far more enthusiasm. She threw her arms around his neck and pulled his head down towards her own to celebrate with a kiss.

* * *

Meanwhile Alan Cannon was moving forwards with renewed energy. The space between the top of the clay and the tunnel roof slowly widened until he could struggle forward on his hands and knees. The tunnel roof was intact at this point and when he stopped for a moment to rest, Cannon could, if he reached above him, feel the reassuring smooth plastic-coated steel sheeting. Despite the fact that there was more room in which to move, Cannon noticed that the going was becoming heavier. His hands and knees were sinking deeper and deeper into the clay and each move forwards required a considerable effort.

Once he found himself face to face with the side wall, having become disorientated in the dark, and after that he moved forwards with his left hand within touching distance of the nearest tunnel wall. He found it strangely reassuring.

The end, when it came, was quite unexpected. The clay had become steadily softer and Cannon had found himself breathing more and more heavily in an attempt to keep going. The space between the top of the mud and the tunnel ceiling was now nearly two feet and Cannon sat back, leaning against the wall, to rest for a moment. That was the mistake which cost him his life. With his weight resting on his buttocks instead of being spread along his legs and arms Cannon found himself sinking deeper and deeper into the clay. He struggled and kicked out but found himself simply sinking more rapidly. In the dark his arms thrashed around and he sank deeper and deeper. The soft bluish clay reached up to his waist and seemed actively to pull him down. Cannon spread his arms widely and tried to spread his legs. His legs, however, were already imprisoned by the clay.

It all took less than five minutes. As Cannon weakened, his arms stopped flailing and then they too sank below the surface of the clay. Soon only his head stayed visible. The clay reached his chin and Cannon, realising that there was no longer any chance of escape, gave up hope. A thin, high-pitched scream echoed along the tunnel, dancing off the walls and ceiling. Then the mud began to trickle into his mouth and ears. Finally it reached his nose and Cannon was slowly suffocated.

A moment or two later the clay closed over the remains of Alan Cannon and his tomb was complete.

2000 hrs. August 6th, Paris

The following statement was distributed by hand to all the leading newspapers and agency offices in Paris.

'At a meeting of the board of the Compagnie de Chemin de Fer Sous-marin Entre La France et L'Angleterre in Paris this evening, it was regretfully decided that the appointment of M.P. Garin as general manager of the company would be terminated as from 2000 hours today (European Standard Time).

'The board, which will be making a new appointment within the next few days, wishes to express sympathy to all those who have friends or relatives involved in the tunnel collapse.

'Every effort will be made to expedite rescue attempts and regular bulletins will be published from his office.

'The cause of the accident is not yet known but independent experts believe the problem was caused by a structural fault.

'The Compagnie de Chemin de Fer Sous-marin Entre La France et L'Angleterre wishes to apologise for the inconvenience caused to its customers by the cancellation of trains. Normal services will be resumed as soon as possible.'

2135 hrs. August 6th, Rescue Team, Channel Tunnel

Garin and Bleriot stood together watching and waiting. The two drilling crews had done far better than anyone had dared to hope. They were both within centimetres of breaking through into the other main tunnel.

'I want to send in two rescue teams with listening equipment,' said Garin. 'We'll get the equipment set up and see just what we can pick up in the way of sound.'

'Where's Raspail?' asked Bleriot. 'Did you see him?'

Garin frowned. 'I thought he was with you,' he said. 'I radioed ahead to the control room asking them to get a message to him.'

Bleriot shook his head.

The duty controller at Sangatte told Garin that they'd sent a message through to Raspail's home, but that his wife had insisted that she hadn't seen him. She had assumed that Raspail had been at work in the tunnel.

'Thanks,' said Garin. He looked across at Bleriot and lifted his hands, palm upwards. 'Better see if anyone has seen him.'

Bleriot spoke hurriedly for a moment into his radio mouthpiece then waited for a moment. He listened, nodded once, acknowledged the message he received over his headphones and then looked across at Garin.

'The driver brought him in hours ago,' he said.

'Where to?'

'He dropped him in the tunnel. Near the blockage.'

Suddenly Garin knew what had happened. 'He'll have to take his chances,' he said, with deliberate brusqueness. 'I can't afford to spare anybody to look for him.'

Bleriot, understanding, said nothing. He turned away and listened to one of the drilling crew foremen who'd been standing a metre away, waiting respectfully but with ill-concealed impatience.

'We're through,' said the foreman. He shook his head sadly. 'I can't see you finding anyone alive,' he added.

Bleriot signalled to the first rescue team to go into the newly opened passageway into the England-bound tunnel. At long last the rescue was under way.

2134 hrs. August 6th, The Tunnel Train

'How long is it?' asked Dr Chatwyn.

'Is what?' enquired Peter Cater.

'Is it since Tambroni got back?'

Cater shrugged his shoulders. 'Why?'

'How long do you think it would take Cannon to get some help?'

Cater shrugged again. The tunnel was now in permanent darkness. They had no more materials with which to make torches. Chatwyn repeated his question.

'Don't know. Suppose it depends on how far he had to go,' said Cater. He was reluctant to talk. The air in their relatively confined space was stuffy and hot, despite the fact that the tunnel

Tambroni and Cannon had dug through the clay acted as a sort of air shaft.

'Perhaps one or two more of us should follow him,' suggested Tambroni. 'I'd rather do something than sit here. I'll go in again.'

'I'll come with you,' said Susan Roberts.

* * *

The two of them emerged, naked except for a covering of sticky blue clay, into the glare of a thousand television and newspaper lights and flashbulbs. Both of them were spattered with Tambroni's blood. The photographers and cameramen had been waiting for nearly eighteen hours and they were hungry for news. The sight of the first two bedraggled survivors emerging from the tunnel attracted the newspaper and television people like a light attracting moths. The Sangatte security officers took twenty-five minutes to extricate them from the crowd.

* * *

The other survivors followed soon after. Mrs Black was supported by her children though now they no longer looked or acted like children; one supporting each of her arms, both were murmuring words of comfort and encouragement.

James Gower, alone, looking as guilty as he felt, furtive, desperate to see his wife again, to beg her forgiveness. Not knowing yet that he would never have the chance. He looked from side to side like a criminal expecting to be spotted, making sure that Hélène was yards away from him.

Hélène didn't mind that. She was already busy planning her future. She would write her story. A magazine piece. A book perhaps. Maybe a film.

Peter Cater wanted only to see his family. He felt glad to be alive, grateful for a second chance. There would be no more photographs. But he did wonder what had happened to the two coins he had thrown into the darkness. Would anyone find them or would they stay buried? He really didn't care. Just wondered.

Dr Chatwyn was more surprised to be alive than relieved. He felt quite pleased with himself. He hadn't let himself down as badly as he would have expected. He was exhausted but walked with more pride and confidence than he had for some time. And then he remembered his friend, Dr Singh, and tears started to roll down his cheeks.

Gaston Raenackers was carried out of the tunnel on a stretcher. There was nothing physically wrong with him. It wasn't that he couldn't walk. He just couldn't find the energy. He had lost the will to move. It would take him a long time to recover from the shame he felt. His body wasn't broken but his spirit was.

And finally, of course, walked Miss Millington, a yard or two behind them all; the least concerned. She even managed a smile. She touched the cheap ring on the third finger of her left hand; started to remove it, and then stopped. She left the ring where it was. Now she couldn't understand why she had not worn it every day of her life. The only certainty was that she would, she knew, wear it with pride until she died. It was all she had that really mattered to her. The ring and her memories. The tunnel workers who helped rescue her, and the journalists who spoke to her afterwards, all marvelled at her resilience. She was, they all agreed, the strongest and most astonishing of all the survivors. They would, perhaps, have been surprised if they had known that she derived her strength from the cheap ring she wore.

PART FOUR

Two weeks after the rescue, Susan Roberts began to feel ill. She visited her doctor on the morning of 20th August.

'I've had headaches and pains in my arms and legs for several days now,' she told him. 'Do you think I've got some sort of virus?'

'You were in that crash in the Channel Tunnel, weren't you?'

Susan nodded. 'I had a full medical afterwards. They said they could find nothing wrong.'

'Well, it's probably just delayed shock,' the doctor smiled, reassuringly. 'Still, I'll have a look at you just to put your mind at rest!'

When he examined her the doctor found to his surprise that she had several spots on her arms and legs. They looked rather like small blisters. There was, in particular, one large spot on her left foot.

'What are they?' asked Susan. 'Has something bitten me?'

'They aren't bites,' said the doctor thoughtfully. 'It rather looks like smallpox or chickenpox.'

'Smallpox!' said Susan Roberts.

'Don't worry!' said the doctor with a smile. 'Smallpox was officially certified as an extinct disease years ago. It can't be that. But although the distribution is very unusual it might just be chickenpox, I'm afraid. Not that we see much of that around these days.'

'What should I do?'

'No need to do anything special,' said the doctor. 'I'll give you some calamine lotion to dab on the spots if they get itchy.'

Susan sighed with relief, picked up her stockings and began

to dress. She did it slowly and provocatively. It was a pity she didn't come to the surgery more often. This doctor wasn't too bad at all.

For a catalogue of Vernon Coleman's books please write to:

Publishing House
Trinity Place
Barnstaple
Devon EX32 9HG
England

Telephone	01271 328892
Fax	01271 328768

Outside the UK:

Telephone	+44 1271 328892
Fax	+44 1271 328768

Or visit our website:

www.vernoncoleman.com